Master Georgie

a novel

Master Georgie

a novel

Beryl Bainbridge

Carroll & Graf Publishers, Inc.
New York

SISKIYOU COUNTY PUBLIC LIBRARY
719 FOURTH STREET
YREKA, CALIFORNIA 96097

For Mike and Parvin Lawrence

Copyright © 1998 by Beryl Bainbridge

First published in England by Gerald Duckworth & Co. Ltd.

First Carroll & Graf edition 1998

Carroll & Graf Publishers, Inc.
19 West 21st Street
New York, NY 10010-6805

Library of Congress Cataloging-in-Publication Data is available.

ISBN: 0-7867-0563-9

Manufactured in the United States of America

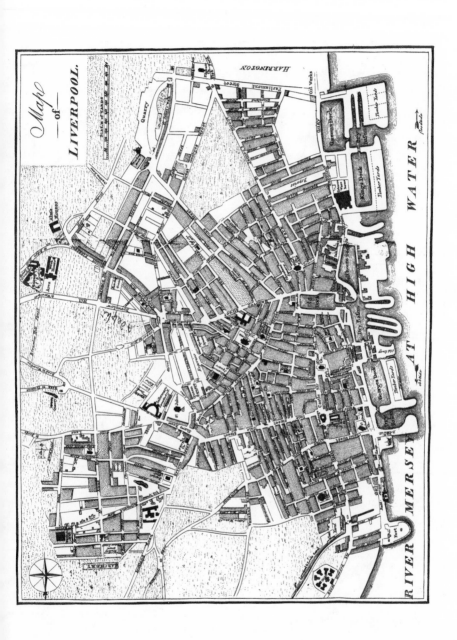

Map of LIVERPOOL.

HARRINGTON

RIVER MERSEY AT HIGH WATER

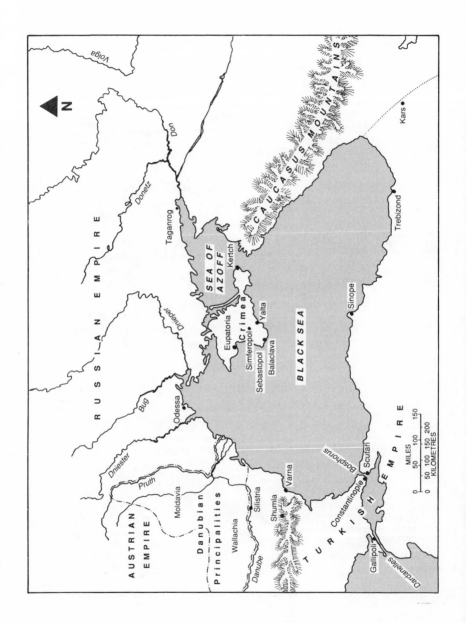

Plate 1. 1846

GIRL IN THE PRESENCE
OF DEATH

I was twelve years old the first time Master Georgie ordered me to stand stock still and not blink. My head was on a level with the pillow and he had me rest my hand on Mr Hardy's shoulder; a finger-tip chill struck through the cloth of his white cotton shirt. It was a Saturday, the feast of the Assumption, and to stop my eyelids from fluttering I pretended God would strike me blind if I let them, which is why I ended up looking so startled. Mr Hardy didn't have to be told to keep still because he was dead.

I say I was twelve years old, but I can't be sure. I don't recollect a mother and never had a birthday until the Hardy family took me in. According to Master Georgie, I'd been found some nine years before, in a cellar in Seel Street, sat beside the body of a woman whose throat had been nibbled by rats.

I didn't have a name, so they called me Myrtle, after the street where the orphanage stands. It was intended I should be placed there, and I would have been if the smallpox hadn't broken out. Instead, a business gentleman on the board of the Liverpool Health Committee and known to Mr Hardy pressed him to house me until the epidemic was over. When this happened and it came time for my departure, Miss Beatrice set up howling; she'd taken a fancy to me. She lost interest the following year when Mr Hardy brought home the dog, but by then Mrs O'Gorman had taken me in hand, so they let me be.

I was fortunate, for I was taught to read by Mrs Hardy, and Mr Hardy sometimes chucked me under the chin and asked how I did. Often, I was allowed to play with Master Freddie, before he went away to school. It was only Mrs O'Gorman who ever beat me, and that for my own good. I was not loved and counted it a blessing; it meant my affections raged undiluted and I could lavish all on Master Georgie.

I don't remember anything about being found. Master Georgie once told me that if I concentrated hard enough the memories might come back, like the images that reared up on his photogenic plates. That scared me, for he performed such magic in the dark, and sometimes, after he'd put the idea into my head, waking at night to the shuffle of leaves along the guttering, I fancied there was a ghastly picture about to imprint itself upon the windowpane. Noticing the shadows under my eyes and ferreting out the cause, Mrs O'Gorman declared he was a wicked boy for spooning me such nonsense.

Twice I went back to that house in Seel Street and stood at the railings. The basement area was flooded and the window glass too grimy to peer through.

That particular afternoon in damp August – the one that ended so curiously – began with Mrs Hardy plummeting into one of her states. I'd been summoned to see to the tiger-skin rug. The dog had got in again and Mrs O'Gorman had shooed me upstairs to stiff-brush its grey hairs from those blazing stripes. Master Georgie and Mrs Hardy were seated at opposite ends of the dining-room table.

I didn't like the tiger; its jaws gaped open and unlike Mr Hardy it didn't have any lids to its eyes, which meant they glared. Mrs Hardy detested the rug as much as I did, though for different reasons. Mr Hardy swore he'd bagged the beast himself, in the Madras Province, in the days when he'd been employed as an overseer of Irrigation Works. It was a boast Mrs Hardy had shaken to fragments on more than one agitated occasion; she spat he'd bought it cheap at Riley's auction rooms in Water Street and carried it home over his shoulder.

The rug was positioned in front of the french windows overlooking the garden and the orchard beyond, so I had my back to the table when Mrs Hardy said, 'Georgie, dear, you won't be going to the Institute today, will you?'

He agreed he wouldn't.

'Though I expect you'll be going out on business.'

Young as I was I sensed this was more in the nature of an accusation than a supposition. The brush turned to stone in my hand. Mrs Hardy frightened me, for she stared so. Often, when her mouth smiled it didn't signify she was pleased. All the same, she had rescued me, taught me my letters, and I didn't want her upset. I fixed my gaze on the plum trees in the orchard. Miss Beatrice was out there, pirouetting under branches laden with round, rotten fruit. Fat Dr Potter stalked her, face raised to the cloudy heavens.

I heard Georgie say, 'Not business, Mother. I'm meeting William Rimmer.'

[11]

'Of course you are,' she replied. 'You men always have friends to see … either that or business to see to.'

There was a silence for a long minute, broken by tapping. I swivelled on my haunches, making believe I was attending to the bony head of the tiger. Mrs Hardy was stabbing at the food on her plate and giving one of her stares, eyes lachrymose with bulging misery; gravy splattered the cloth. Master Georgie had explained to me that the stare was peculiar to a malfunction of the thyroid, a gland common to us all, only in Mrs Hardy's case it had started growing. As for her misery, why, that was all due to her husband; she was a neglected wife. Mr Hardy had promised to come home at midday and already it was five after three by the clock on the mantelshelf.

Master Georgie rose then and stooped to kiss his mother on the cheek. She jerked her head away and he made a small mew of annoyance.

'For pity's sake,' she whined, 'help me, for I can't help myself.'

'I don't know how to, Mother,' he said, and the defeated slump of his shoulders pierced me to the quick.

Usually he offered to stay with her when she was out of sorts, and almost always she told him not to be foolish. This time he didn't utter a word. He just stood there, looking down at her tear-stained face. She was harder on him than on either Master Freddie or Miss Beatrice. It was because he was her first born and she'd been torn to pieces before he plopped out. Mrs O'Gorman told me that. I didn't doubt he loved her still, but those childhood days when he could show clinging proof of it had gone for ever.

[12]

She said bitterly, 'Don't look so worried, Georgie. You mustn't let my little misfortunes spoil your day,' to which he retorted with equal bitterness, 'To hear is to obey.' I ran out of the room because I couldn't bear it any longer.

The hall kept changing from dark to light as clouds ran over the sun. When I dragged the plug of dog hairs from the brush a current of air from the leaded window whirled it, dandelion fashion, up the well of the stairs to circle the antlers of the stag's head on the landing.

The evening before, Mrs O'Gorman had trapped me in the scullery to acquaint me with the Assumption. She said someone had to school me, seeing I was being raised in such a Godless house. That was a dig at Dr Potter, for being under the sway of the new sciences. Dr Potter held that the world wasn't created in six days; it was more like thousands of years. Why, even mountains hadn't always stayed in the same place. St James' Mount, which overlooks the sunken cemetery, may once have been a flat stretch of earth, grassless under a sheet of ice.

It didn't worry me like it did Mrs O'Gorman, who moaned that it wasn't for the likes of her to doubt the permanency of rocks. But then, her rock was the Kingdom of Heaven and she didn't want it shifted.

She'd pinned me to the chair at the scullery table and trumpeted that tomorrow was a special day, one on which the body of Our Lord's mother had been wafted up to heaven to be united with her soul. The worms hadn't got to her like they will with me, on account of Our Lord loving her so. I only half believed her.

Above me, the web of hair began to drift apart. I mouthed

He loves me, he loves me not, though I wasn't thinking of Our Lord.

Presently Master Georgie emerged and began to button himself into his outdoor coat. His fur-lined cloak, the one I tugged out later, hung abandoned in the hall closet. He'd left off wearing it because Mr Hardy, returning merry with drink from mornings at the Corn Exchange, had cried out once too often, *'O Vanitas vanitatem.'*

A noise of busted china came from the dining room. Master Georgie flinched; Mrs Hardy's heart was in pieces for the umpteenth time and she was taking it out on the dinner plates. A sunbeam pierced the fanlight above the front door, painting his hair with silver.

Just then, Mrs O'Gorman came up the basement stairs and said calmly enough, 'You be on your way, Master Georgie. No sense both of us being put upon.'

He dithered for a moment, during which time Mrs Hardy, wailing like a banshee, rushed from the dining room and clambered clumsily up the stairs. Mrs O'Gorman stood her ground, her face giving nothing away. The sun went in again and Master Georgie faded. Looking across the hall he crooked his finger for me to follow.

I did as he bid, running behind him as he marched down the drive and strode the blackberry-hedged lane leading to Prince's Boulevard. I threw Mrs O'Gorman's sweeping brush into the nettles. He didn't look back, but then, why should he? I was his shadow. He swung his arms like a soldier and his boots splashed mud.

Master Georgie needed me with him so that he could enjoy himself without becoming jittery over conditions at home. If the afternoon proved convivial and he wanted to stay out for supper, I'd be required to run off to see how the land lay with his mother. If Dr Potter had given her one of his powders or Mr Hardy had come home, I had no cause to return. If she was still under her black clouds I'd have to hare back to fetch him.

Along the Boulevard, under the summer trees, nurse-maids wheeled their infants out. Earlier there had been a downpour and small girls screamed as sudden gusts of wind scattered raindrops on their heads. The Punch and Judy man was setting up his box alongside the carriage stop. Already the Jew-boy employed to gather a crowd was squeezing on his accordion. The horse that pulled the purple van stood tossing its nose in its feed-bag.

No one I knew had ever set eyes on the man who jiggled Mr Punch into life. Some said he was a dwarf and others that he was nine foot high. He fixed up his stall against the doors of the van and crept in from behind, so as to keep up the illusion. Besides, when it came time for the Jew-boy to pass round the hat, we children generally melted away. The dog Toby was real; he nipped at your ankles if you tried to crawl under the front cloth.

I loitered, waiting for the striped curtains to open. The best bit was always when Judy went off to collect the washing and Mr Punch started thwacking the baby to make it leave off bawling – then the young folk broke out shrieking and sniggering, particularly those that got whipped regularly.

I didn't fret over Master Georgie going on ahead. I knew I'd find him at the Washington Hotel where he was meeting his friend, William Rimmer, a fellow student at the Medical Institute.

The curtains had just been pushed sideways to reveal Mr Punch leant over the cradle, swinging the bellowing baby back and forth, when the accident happened. There was a sudden hiss from the crowd, a surge backwards and a shower of droplets from above as the stall tipped through the lower branches of the trees and toppled to the ground. Mr Punch fell out altogether and lay in a lump in the puddles. Dog Toby jumped and snarled, jumped and yapped.

It was all over in a blink of an eye. Then, wonder of wonders, the Punch and Judy man reared up before us, scrambling to his feet and waving his arms to fight off the flapping fold of the candy-striped front cloth. From his mouth flew a stream of oaths, which came out comical, not fearsome, for he still used that parrot voice. Beneath his sodden top hat his nose curved down to meet his chin.

The van with its golden letters on the side hadn't suffered so much as a scratch, though it had been shoved a foot or more towards the crowd, thus rocking the stall from its support. In the uproar, a lad ran off with the Jew-boy's accordion but a woman hit him over the head with her gamp, at which he howled and let it drop. She was comical too, for as she whacked at him she squawked out, 'Who's a naughty boy, then?', imitating Mr Punch when chastising the baby. We children fairly burst with laughter, skipping about in the wet with the dog Toby snapping at our legs.

The incident was explained and settled satisfactorily enough, the gentleman responsible for the hoo-ha fishing out money to cover the damage. At cock-crow, so it was said, a vegetable cart had spilled cabbages on to the road, all of which, save one, had been recovered or run off with. The gentleman's horse, who had seen service with a cavalry regiment, mistaking it for a puff-adder, had reared up and crashed down sideways, striking the van with its flank.

The animal had recently returned from Africa, where puff-adders were quite common. They hadn't any teeth but if they bit you their tongues imparted a poison that could turn your blood to treacle.

Presently, the gentleman climbed back on to his horse and trotted away, after which the Punch and Judy man bundled his dismembered box into the van and shut up shop for the day. He was still swearing, though not so loudly as before.

*

It began to rain before I reached the Washington Hotel. I hadn't my shawl, but a spot of damp was nothing to me. In winter, when the wind howled up from the river, I huddled in the doorway of the Star Theatre. Once, an actor came by and said I was pretty and why didn't I come inside to get warm by the Green Room fire. I didn't go because the rouge on his cheeks made him look more angry than kindly. Besides, I knew he was buttering me, the line of my mouth being too determined for prettiness and my eyes too deeply set, which lends me a melancholy look. Another time, in December, my feet turned quite blue and Mrs O'Gorman had to rub them with goose-fat to restore the circulation. What did I care! I'd freeze stiff for Master Georgie.

In summer, my favourite place was on the granite steps of the entrance to the railway station in Lime Street. From there I could see down the slope to where the hotel stood within its square of garden, the red roses bobbing tall in the wind. On clear days, beneath high blue heavens, the humps of the Welsh hills rode the horizon. Now, the grey river met the grey sky, and a low white sun, sliced by the masts of ships, sailed through a splash of scarlet petals.

Mr Hardy had an oil painting of the same view hung on his study wall. The masts were there, and the row of cottages sloping down towards the tobacco warehouse, but the Washington was missing because it hadn't been built. It was a very old painting and had belonged to Mr Hardy's father, yet the colours were as fresh as new, unlike Master Georgie's photographic pictures which turned black after a week.

I had been sitting for an hour or more, watching the people bustling back and forth, the smoke from the steam engines spurting into the lowering skies, when I witnessed a Christian act. A woman who had been standing at the bottom of the steps, a child in her arms and a wicker basket at her feet, was approached by another woman, better dressed than she and holding her skirts up from the wet. A live duck sat squashed in the basket, its neck tied to the handle, its beak bound with string. The woman pulled back her shawl so as to show off the baby nestling at her breast. Just then a boy sneaked through the crowd and snatching up the basket ran off with it. Unaware, the woman went on cooing. Seconds later, another boy appeared at her elbow and deposited the basket back at her feet. He didn't utter a word. Straightening up, he caught me watching him. He was three or four years older than myself, dark of complexion, either from dirt or nature, and his mouth was disfigured by what I took to be an epithelioma of the upper lip. I noticed such things because Master Georgie let me read his medical books, though, as yet, I didn't understand them perfectly.

At that instant William Rimmer came out of the hotel. I waited until I saw Master Georgie emerge, then sped down the steps, across the square and into the doorway of the Union Warehouse. Master Georgie got irritated if I hung about too closely. I couldn't hear what they were saying, but from the agitated manner in which William Rimmer walked off a few paces, then returned, I gathered they were arguing rather than talking. Mostly, they discussed cadavers and blood vessels and the like, so I reckoned it was a medical rift. All the same, Master Georgie looked hang- dog, which was out of character, and I felt a sudden flutter of distress. Gauging they were too locked to notice, I stole nearer and hid behind the roses. It was still raining and water sprayed from Master Georgie's hat.

William Rimmer said, 'I won't listen to your excuses.'

Master Georgie said, 'I have nothing to excuse.' He spoke calmly, which was his way. He held that if a man wanted his judgement to be accepted, it should be expressed coolly and without passion.

'You can't deny it was underhand,' said William Rimmer. 'Damn it, George, you knew my feelings.'

'In the circumstances, I don't see I was at fault. You heard what Mrs Prescott said ... What was I to do? ... Was I supposed to refuse so that you could step in?'

'In your place I would have done – '

'Would you indeed? And risk appearing boorish?'

'It wasn't the action of a friend,' William Rimmer stormed, and with that he walked off again, only this time he kept straight on and didn't look back.

Master Georgie hesitated and then made as if to follow. After no more than a few yards he changed his mind and almost ran across the square. He didn't turn to see if I was at his heels.

I couldn't think what the quarrel was about. Mrs Prescott was a wealthy woman who lived in grand style beyond Strawberry Fields. She had three daughters, two of whom were rumoured to be plain and the third handsome. I'd heard Mr Hardy remark on her looks, and he was a great man for knowing what constituted a good-looking woman. Mrs Prescott had given a dance the week before to which Master Georgie had been invited. By the sound of it, so had William Rimmer. Beyond that, it was a mystery what Mrs Prescott had said and what Master Georgie had done that William Rimmer considered underhand.

My mind wouldn't let the matter rest, the argumentative words tumbling over and over in my head as I trailed Master Georgie the length of Bold Street. It was monstrous of William Rimmer to upbraid him. Why, when he'd caught an infection of the finger from slicing livers in the dissecting room, and lain at death's door for two days, groaning under the fever, Master Georgie had spent a whole night sitting up

with him. On his return, recounting to Mrs Hardy the tor-
ment his friend was enduring, tears swelled up in his eyes.
It hurt my heart to have his devotion so easily forgotten.

Master Georgie should have turned left when we reached
St John's Church; instead he swerved right, up the cobbled
rise towards St James' Mount. I reckon he was lost in
thought, either that or putting time between himself and
home. It had stopped raining and a watery sun floated
above the chimney stacks. Mrs O'Gorman didn't like setting
foot in this part of the town. Poverty, she confided, sent her
skittering, due to her having nudged too close to it on
account of Ireland and the potatoes.

Years past, when Mr Hardy's father was alive, merchants
lived in the streets nearest to their manufacturing busi-
nesses beside the river. It was expansion, Master Georgie
said, and the inrush of humanity, that sent them scuttling
upwards to build their mansions in the hills. The once
pampered houses now stood in mouldering disarray, balco-
nies rusted, windows stuffed with rags. Sometimes the
crowded cellars flooded and infants drowned along with
the rats. Such disasters afforded Mrs Hardy solace, for on
her good days she attended committees for the relief of the
poor, which took her out of herself.

Miss Beatrice, in a spiteful mood, had implied that I too
might have crawled in from the bogs of Ireland. She crowed
that when found I had a scrap of green ribbon rotting in my
hair. Mrs O'Gorman said it wasn't true. She'd been the one
to cut my hair off to be rid of the lice, so she should know. I
didn't mind one way or the other. It was of no interest to me
where I came from, only where I was going.

All the same, I quickened my pace as Master Georgie climbed the pavement of Mount Street. Poor people appear predatory owing to their bones showing, and bones were in abundance among the gaggle of ragged boys on the corner, the wild children squabbling in the gutter, the stupefied men slouched against the railings. They didn't molest me for they saw I had nothing to give. A woman accosted Master Georgie but he waved her aside, not from lack of charity, simply from his being abstracted. Of average height, stout of build, he walked with feet turned out and back straight as a ramrod. I watched the way he swung his arms. How strange it is that even a mode of walking can inspire love.

Suddenly he shouted over his shoulder, 'Don't lag behind, Myrtle. Keep up with me.' For perhaps thirty seconds, until that scuffed front door opened, framing a screaming woman clad in a torn chemise, I was happy, for his flung injunction signified he knew I was there and didn't want me lost.

The face of the woman in the doorway was distorted with fright. She had few teeth and her mouth resembled a dark hole. Master Georgie was about to pass by when she screamed again, shrill and menacing as a swooping gull. The sound stopped him momentarily in his tracks. He looked about him to see who would come to her aid – but what did a scream amount to in such a wretched place? Mounting the cracked steps he followed her into the house.

I scampered after, not wishing to miss the excitement. As the woman toiled ahead up the stairs I could see black hairs bristling on her plump white calves; breath needed for the ascent, she'd ceased uttering those ghastly bird cries. Someone climbed the stairs behind me and when I looked over my shoulder I was astonished to see the boy who earlier had rescued the duck. I half stumbled; the banister rail on the turn of the landing was broken and a splinter of wood pierced my palm as I propelled myself upwards.

We came at last to an open door on the third floor. Master Georgie and the woman entered the room while I remained on the threshold. I could see a fire burning in the grate, its reflection flickering upon the rails of a brass bed. Close by stood a little round table bearing a bottle, a glass and a pocket watch. On the bed, face down, arms stretched above the head, both hands clenched in a fist about the bars, lay a figure clad in nothing but a shirt, naked buttocks exposed. It was a curious position to sleep in, for he appeared to hang rather than lie, back arched as though gathering momentum like the man on the flying trapeze. I knew it was a man because his breeches hung from the knob of the bed.

Another harsh cry rang through the room, and it was worse than anything the woman had managed, for this time it came from Master Georgie. Startled, I was about to edge closer when the duck-boy pushed me aside and demanded, 'What's wrong, Margaret? Trouble, is it?'

'He died on me,' the woman wailed. 'It weren't nothing to do with me.'

Master Georgie fell to his knees beside the bed. He made no attempt to turn the body over or feel a pulse; poking a finger out he traced the fold of the shirt where it rucked at the neck. It had gone very quiet and a feeling of dread began to steal over me, as though something horrible was about to happen in that darkening room with the watch ticking and glinting on the table.

At last Master Georgie looked up and the dread became palpable, for his face was drained of colour and his eyes as bewildered as my own. I ran to him then and put my hand on his shoulder, and though I don't believe he knew who it was, for a fleeting moment he inclined his head and rested his cheek against my wrist. Then he shrugged away and stood up.

'We must move him,' he said, addressing the boy. 'You must help me move him.' He was pleading rather than asking.

'Is it to the Infirmary?' the boy wanted to know, at which Master Georgie shouted out, 'God damn you, no.' After which outburst, visibly struggling to gain control of himself, he added more reasonably, 'I know this gentleman. It will be kinder to his family if I take him to his house.'

Seeing me standing there he ordered the woman to put me into another room. 'I ain't got no other room,' she said. All the same, she hustled me on to the landing and endeavoured to shut the door in my face, only I fought her and she gave up. She had no power in her arms and her breath stank of drink.

It took strength to unclasp the hands from the bed rail and turn the body over. Quick as a flash Georgie pulled down its shirt, for decency's sake. And now it was my turn to cry out, for it was Mr Hardy who lay there, grey hair lank as seaweed, lips purple as the plums in his orchard.

The woman came to me then and whispered, 'Who is he, dearie?' but I stayed mute. She tugged at my hair to make

[24]

me tell, and I never even whimpered. She could have pulled out every hair on my head and still I wouldn't have told, for that would have been a betrayal.

'I need a conveyance to take him home,' Master Georgie said.

The boy nodded in the direction of the window. 'There's a van out in the alleyway and a horse in the stables. I'll need money.'

'I have money,' said Master Georgie, digging into his pockets.

The woman had sidled closer to the bed, her eyes concentrating on the watch on the table. I guessed what she was about and darting forward snatched it up and held it fiercely to my chest. She struck at me, catching me a blow on the ear which sent me tumbling backwards on to the bed. My leg touched Mr Hardy's ankle and its fading warmth sent such a shock through me that I jerked upright as though galvanised by lightning.

I gave the watch to Master Georgie. He was standing at the window looking on to the alleyway below. He took it without acknowledgement, flopping it over and over in his cupped hands. So as to be less noticeable I sat on the floor with my back to the stained wallpaper.

Presently, the duck-boy returned. He said the horse was being put into harness and we should go out the back way, through the scullery and into the yard. Master Georgie said, 'Good, good,' and stared down at the bed. Plucking the trousers from off the brass rail he began to steer Mr Hardy's feet into the funnels of cloth; there were corns round as beads embossed on his white toes.

The woman, her assistance required, flapped her hands and shrank away. I stood up, prepared to help, but the boy got there before me. When they humped the breeches over Mr Hardy's backside, his shirt rolled up and I was taken by surprise at the limpness of his private parts. I'd seen them before, one Easter when he'd felt compelled to show them me, only that time a thing rigid as a carrot had stuck out between his fingers.

Master Georgie and the boy carried him down between them. He was a well-built man and his weight sank him in the middle. The woman, who had been given money to open up the yard, defaulted and scuttled back into the room, whining she had palpitations. I was clutching Mr Hardy's boots, and when his hat tipped off on the bend in the stairs I harvested that too. His eyes were closed but his mouth sagged open, from his being jogged.

I had to squeeze past to unlock the scullery door into the back. Once it was ajar, the light of the waning afternoon caught our faces. Master Georgie's cheeks had flushed pink again, though that was due to exertion. The gate into the alleyway was insecure on its hinges and had been nailed shut to hold it fast. Master Georgie and the boy swarmed over the wall to look for something that might serve as a battering ram to burst it open. They sat Mr Hardy against the stump of a sycamore tree and told me to keep an eye on him, as though he was likely to stroll away. I did, yet I kept my distance, watching the rain glistening on the buttons of his coat.

Until he was dead I'd liked Mr Hardy. He was cheerful and lacking in malice and on the few occasions he'd noticed me his eyes twinkled. At parties he always sang after his dinner, and you could hear his voice all over the house. It was usually the same song, about a little drummer boy who called for his mother as he lay dying on a battlefield, and when it was over and the guests clapped their appreciation he sang it again. It had very sad words but he bellowed so heartily when it came to the line, *Mother dear, I am fading fast*, that no one could forbear laughing.

Now, if proof were required that the soul flees the body, I might have pointed the finger at him; there was no mistaking his emptiness. For his sake I hoped Mrs O'Gorman had been in the right of it when she'd asserted that rich people always had a friend waiting for them beyond the bright blue sky; he was no great shakes without his cronies round him. Standing there, listening to the melancholy gurglings of roof-top pigeons, I dwelt with pleasure on the unstable and transitory nature of life, seeing I was fortunate enough to be alive. Although the better part of me felt distress, I did know that I revelled in the moment. The mind, like the eye, perceives things more clearly in daylight.

There was a sudden thud against the gate, though it merely shuddered, and then two more blows, after which it gave and swung wide. Outside stood the purple van with its letters gaudily outlined in gold. It wasn't the Punch and Judy man's beast between the shafts, for that was no bigger than a donkey and this was the size of one of the dray horses that thundered from the cobbled courtyard of the brewery.

I held open the van doors while Master Georgie and the duck-boy lugged Mr Hardy across the yard. Once the boy stopped to catch his breath and Master Georgie cried out,

'Hurry ... we must lay him flat.' Possibly the boy thought this levelling was required out of respect, but I knew haste was a necessity, owing to the danger of rigor mortis taking a grip. It wouldn't do to have Mr Hardy arrive home shaped like a jack-knife.

The interior of the van still held the twisted remains of the puppet box, though Mr Punch wasn't there, or Judy or the constable. We had to push the lengths of wood to one side to make space, and when it was done and the stiffening legs were straightened I was urged to jump in. Master Georgie was going to sit up with the boy, to give him directions. I didn't care for the arrangement, but before I could demur the doors were slammed shut, the outside bolt pulled to, and Mr Hardy and I sank into a blackness as impenetrable as the tomb.

The journey was a bumpy affair, the van being light and the horse powerful. I had to put my legs across Mr Hardy and press down hard to keep him pinned flat. When the wheels hit holes in the road we fairly bounced in the air; flying round a corner a sharp object hit me in the chest. Reading it with my fingers, I recognised Mr Punch's poor baby and stroked its wooden cheek against my own, crooning it mustn't be afraid.

In the darkness, pictures floated in my head of Mrs Hardy and Miss Beatrice becoming acquainted with the dreadful news. Miss Beatrice was weeping, for herself rather than her departed father, because now he was gone she'd have to stay with her widowed mother and give up the idea of running away to sea. Mrs O'Gorman blamed education for putting the notion into her head, because she'd never pined for anything so outlandish until she was sent away to boarding school in Lichfield. Mrs Hardy was lying in bed calling out for Dr Potter to fetch the port wine. He was too occupied in comforting Miss Beatrice to pay heed, for she was in his arms at last, and his face, loony with delight, beamed above her trembling shoulder. I poured out the wine from the cooler on the dresser and took it to Mrs Hardy; before she sipped she seized my wrist and murmured with popping eyes, 'You are the only true friend I have in this dark world.' I replied, 'It is my duty,' which struck me as not friendly enough, so I added, 'and my pleasure.'

Just then, Mr Hardy rolled under my legs. I was frightened his face might get splinters from the lengths of wood, though I imagined dead flesh needed no protection against the arrows of life. All the same, I tugged at his jacket to bring him closer; it was Master Georgie I was shielding.

Tears had sprung into my eyes when I'd thought about Mrs Hardy, for I reckoned she loved her husband in spite of all her moanings to the contrary, and I expect things were different between them when they were first joined. She was cleverer than him and didn't like his singing and perhaps that had driven them apart. Mrs O'Gorman said they'd met at a horse race in India, where it was so hot that everyone's judgements got muzzy and they had to lie down every afternoon. It was a question of old habits dying hard, for Mrs Hardy did that even if the weather was cold.

Suddenly the van slowed to a halt and then unaccountably bucked backwards. I could hear the horse's great hooves ringing on the cobblestones as I tipped towards the doors. After some manoeuvring we lurched to the left, which slid me forward again. I don't know where Mr Hardy was and didn't care. I drew my knees up to my chin and gabbled over and over that the Lord was my shepherd and I should not want.

Some minutes later, during which we swayed over rough ground, the vehicle juddered to a stop. The bolt was pulled back and no sooner had I scrambled down, blinking in the light, than Master Georgie took me by the arm and drawing me to one side began to whisper urgent instructions.

'There's a carriage at the front of the house, Myrtle ... use the back stairs and see where Mrs O'Gorman and the servants are ... find out what room Miss Beatrice is in ...'

While his breath deliciously quivered against the rim of my ear, far away on the horizon a smudge of smoke blew from the engine box of a scuttling train.

'... Return as soon as you can ... keep a sharp watch on the garden in case that fool Potter is still mooning about the orchard. Don't let anyone see you, and if they do, don't utter a word of what has happened.'

'I won't,' I said.

'It's a fair trudge to the house,' observed the duck-boy. 'We need something to carry him in.'

'Not a single word,' repeated Master Georgie, looking as though his life depended on it. 'Do you understand?'

'Trust me,' I said. 'My lips are sealed,' and with that I was off, running across the pig field at the side of the house, skirting the fierce rooting sow with the cruel pink eyes, leaping the ditch that ran beside the walled garden.

Mrs O'Gorman was slumped in her chair by the kitchen

fire, pinny over her head to keep out what remained of the light. She dozed soundly, the white fabric flaring in and out as she snored, her hand clutching a slice of toasted bread; the dog had its nose on her knee, licking off the butter. I could hear the cook and the maid-servant chirruping above the clatter of pots in the scullery beyond. One exclaimed, 'Oh, he never, he never,' and the other screeched, 'He did. Yes, he did.'

Creeping up the back stairs I peered out into the hall. There was a bluebottle spinning round and round beneath the chandelier, and what with the whine of its dizzy spirals and the thumping of my heart, I didn't immediately detect the buzz of voices droning from within the parlour. Not daring to go too close, for the door was ajar, I tiptoed as far as the grandfather clock and listened from there. I caught only snatches of the conversation and none of it made sense.

'It's true, I promise you ... all the way home.' That was Miss Beatrice speaking.

Then another voice, one I didn't recognise, pleaded, 'Did he? Are you sure?'

'Hand on my heart ... look into my eyes – '

'I beg you not to be swayed by sisterly feelings – '

'I assure you it's the truth. All that is required is a little feminine cunning.'

'Of which you have more than enough to spare,' interjected a masculine voice, that of Dr Potter and remarkably bitter in tone.

There followed an interchange concerning a proposed tea party, the prospect of which seemed greatly to excite the unseen and unknown young woman, for she cried out, 'You're sure he can be persuaded to come?'

Miss Beatrice said, 'You may depend upon it ... although he always has his nose in a book – '

'Oh dear,' came the response, 'perhaps I should go home and read one at once – ' at which both the speaker and Miss Beatrice squealed with laughter.

'Poor boy,' observed Dr Potter gloomily. 'I fear he is doomed,' and with that the door was flung wide and the hall became loud with the swish of skirts. I was out from behind the clock in a flash and into the clothes cupboard.

They stood by the front door for an age, kissing and exchanging pleasantries, though I could tell Miss Beatrice's interest was beginning to flag. Her voice declined in fervour and shortly, the rain having temporarily ceased, she declared that 'dear Annie' should make haste to her carriage. Dr Potter said he would escort her along the drive but Miss Beatrice cut in and said there was no need. Finally the door slammed shut. There followed a silence broken by a slight scuffle. Dr Potter said, 'You must think I'm made of stone,' and Miss Beatrice said, 'I might prefer it if you were.' Then their footsteps retreated in the direction of the parlour and I heard the door close.

Snatching Master Georgie's fur-lined cloak from off its hook, I sped down the stairs, along the passage and out into the garden. In my flight the cloak swung out at the holly-hocks beside the water-closet wall, sending the withered petals flying. The orchard had dimmed now, the shadows swaying beneath my feet. I misjudged the width of the ditch and trod its muddy depths. Bedraggled, I sprinted across the field to where the Punch and Judy van stood waiting.

The duck-boy sat on a bank of earth, head back, with Master Georgie standing over him, engaged in examining the mulberry stain on his lip. I expect it kept his mind off things to play the doctor. When I approached he took the cloak from me without comment, though its hem was soaked. He neither thanked nor scolded, which made me sullen, for either praise or censure would have been some indication of my existence. I told him that the visitor was gone and that Miss Beatrice and Dr Potter were sparring in the parlour. I didn't have to report on Mrs Hardy, slumber being her regular afternoon activity. 'Mrs O'Gorman,' I said, 'has nodded off. I don't believe she'll stir for a good half-hour or more.'

'Who was the visitor?' he asked.

'A young lady,' I said. 'She's sweet on someone Miss Beatrice knows.'

'Keep an eye on the house,' he ordered, and I wandered away and watched from afar as he and the duck-boy lumped Mr Hardy out of the van and laid him in the cloak. Slung thus, he was carried across the field. At the start his boots and his hat were balanced on his chest, only they kept sliding off. I ran back to help but Master Georgie waved me aside and finally the duck-boy jammed the hat on his own head. I don't know what happened to the boots, for I never saw them again and possibly they're still lying mildewed in the ditch.

Wading ahead through the wet grass, my thoughts became melancholy. The hidden sun was beginning to set now, staining the scudding clouds with crimson, and I took its bloody aspect for an omen. I didn't like Mr Hardy being dead, because it meant my life would be different than before. I tried to bear in mind the example of King David, who, as long as his son lay on a bed of sickness, implored Jehovah to let him live, and when he didn't, snapped his fingers and thought no more of it. Everything that happens, I told myself, is the result of necessity, and therefore inevitable. It was of little comfort.

They got Mr Hardy into the house and up to the second floor without mishap, and deposited him on his bed in the blue room at the end of the passage. Mrs Hardy didn't often allow him into the master bedroom one floor below, owing to headaches and differences of opinion. Mr Hardy's chamber was a man's room, devoid of furbelows and knick-knacks apart from a china vase which his mother had cherished and a pennant belonging to the 52nd Light Infantry that an uncle had carried at Waterloo.

Mr Hardy's hands and face were streaked with dirt from his recent journey, and I was dispatched to bring up water from the kitchens. There was a full pitcher on the dresser but Master Georgie had his wits about him and said it would arouse suspicion if it was found to have been used; Mr Hardy wasn't a great man for washing.

The cook and Lolly, the maid-servant, were sat at the table playing cards. Mrs O'Gorman was awake, though still in her chair. She wanted to know where I'd been and I replied truthfully that I'd followed Master Georgie into town. Before she could question me further I complained of thirst and once in the scullery filled up a basin and took it out by the side door and in through the front. In my haste, half of the water got spilled, but by good fortune Dr Potter was busy tickling the ivories and the parlour door remained shut.

The duck-boy had gone when I returned, and shortly after, when Master Georgie told me to pull up the window – I reckon he was concerned about Mr Hardy's approaching decay – I saw the purple van bouncing along the path beside the pig field.

Soon Mr Hardy looked peaceful enough, clothes brushed, hair combed back, cheek to the pillow so as to keep his mouth closed, one fist prised open, the other thumped against his chest. He had died with his eyes shut, either from pain or not wanting to confront what was coming, so he didn't need pennies on his lids. He was laid out on top of the counterpane, to foster the illusion he'd thrown himself down after a rollicking visit to the Roscoe Club. When we were done I threw the dirty water out of the window and Master Georgie ferreted out a second pair of boots and positioned them under the wicker chair by the wardrobe.

He said, 'Remember, Myrtle, he died in bed from a cessation of the heart.' It was, after all, no more than the truth, if one didn't dwell on which particular bed.

Just as we were quitting the room, a cabbage butterfly flittered in through the open window and settled on Mr Hardy's naked foot. I made to chase it away but Master Georgie stayed my hand. 'Think, Myrtle,' he said, 'of the contrast between what is fleeting and what is permanent.' He was weeping, though silently. Afterwards, he went straight to the stables and, saddling his horse, cantered into the gloaming.

When the gong was beaten for dinner and Mr Hardy didn't appear, it was assumed he was out. It was the maid-servant who found him, an hour or so later, having gone upstairs to see to the fires. She was too shocked to scream and broke the news in a whisper. She told the cook she thought his toes moved, but it was a trick of the candle flame. I was sent off to bring back Dr Potter who had only just left.

I witnessed some of what followed and won't forget it; Miss Beatrice dashing her head against the metal petals circling the oval mirror in the drawing room, pummelling Dr Potter with her fists as he attempted to mop her bleeding brow with his handkerchief; Mrs O'Gorman kicking the dog for scratching at the lino outside the blue room; Mrs Hardy, composed and quiet as the grave, standing in the hall and staring at the front door as though she expected her husband might yet come home.

Around midnight, Master Georgie returned, accompanied by a distant relative of Mrs Hardy's, a Captain Tuckett, who happened to be staying in the neighbourhood. Dr Potter took them upstairs to the drawing room to tell them about Mr Hardy, so I didn't see Master Georgie aping surprise. Mrs Hardy stayed below, and when Captain Tuckett came down again to proffer his condolences, she nodded in a business-like way and turned her back on him. He stood a moment, looking suitably sorrowful, then he put on his hat and took himself off. When I told Mrs O'Gorman she said Captain Tuckett had gained notoriety in bringing an action against the Earl of Cardigan for taking a pot-shot at him on Wimbledon Common, and in any case was so distantly connected to Mrs Hardy that he scarcely counted.

The comings and goings went on into the small hours, though I was sent to my bed. I didn't fall asleep until it was almost light, which was odd seeing I'd been run off my feet.

*

The maid-servant woke me the next morning, shaking my shoulder and urging me to get up. I opened my eyes to a flood of light and the noise of bird-song. Each pane of glass in the window held a square of cloudless sky.

'You're wanted downstairs,' Lolly said. 'Master Georgie needs you in the blue room. By the state of him, he hasn't been to his bed all night.'

He appeared just the same to me – that sweet mouth, those wide apart eyes whose gaze never looked, merely flickered over me; but then, I didn't suppose I saw him as he really was, and never had. He had his camera set up and all his trays placed about the floor. A globule of quicksilver had spilled on to the carpet, where it flashed in the sunlight.

When I glanced at the bed, the events of the day before, until that moment indistinct as a faded dream, returned in odious detail. Mr Hardy had shrunk and his skin grown blotchy, like fruit left too long in the bowl. Someone had kept vigil round him in the night: tears of congealed wax bobbled the stems of the silver candlesticks.

Master Georgie said, 'You and I share a secret, Myrtle. I blame myself for burdening you with it.'

[37]

'I won't tell,' I said.

'I should never have made you a party to it – '

'Wild horses wouldn't make me tell,' I insisted.

'I don't wish you to lie, Myrtle. That would be wrong.' He was fitting his plates into his camera as he spoke, fingers stained yellow from the iodine mixture. 'I'm not worried on my account. It's my mother I have to protect.'

It puzzled me what it was Mrs Hardy needed protecting from. After all, it wasn't the first time Mr Hardy had been carried home the worse for wear, though certainly it was his last.

'Am I to be sent away?' I asked, and my voice trembled at the enormity of the question.

He didn't answer, being occupied in adjusting his tripod. I knew that speed was of the essence once the plate was slotted into the camera, and struggled to be patient. When he was satisfied all was ready, he tugged at my arm and positioned me at the head of the bed. 'Put your hand on his shoulder,' he bid.

'Am I to be sent away?' I repeated, and he replied with some irritation, 'No, Myrtle, no. All I ask is that you hide what you know. It wouldn't do for Mrs O'Gorman to learn of the facts.'

'I don't tell Mrs O'Gorman most things,' I protested. 'Not even when she whips me.'

'Lower your voice,' he begged. 'Walls have ears.' Then he added mysteriously, 'Things will be different from now on … you'll see. We won't go on as before. Now, incline your head … a trifle more … stretch out your fingers … you're bidding him farewell.'

I was saying goodbye to a stranger, because the figure on the bed no longer resembled Mr Hardy. His mouth was a thin, grim line and there were hairs crinkling out from the nostrils of his mottled nose. I could smell something pungent, a combination of iodine and honeysuckle, and wrinkled my own.

'Stop that,' Master Georgie ordered. 'Stand stock still. Don't blink.'

I fixed my gaze on the dead man and told myself God would strike me blind if my eyelids quivered. So intense was my concentration, it was only Master Georgie who breathed in that sun-dappled room. Outside, the birds continued to twitter. All my life, I thought, I will stand at your side; and then I did blink, for the grandness of such a notion welled up tears in my eyes.

Plate 2. 1850

A VEIL LIFTED

George Hardy had called at my lodgings on his way home from the Infirmary. He'd wanted to know whether I was willing to work for him the following morning. I'd replied I was.

'I suggest you be at the house at five o'clock,' he said.

That was just his manner of speaking. Had I taken it simply as a suggestion and arrived five minutes later he would have bitten my head off. Most people thought of him as bookish and of a saintly disposition, but I knew better. He'd said he could promise me an interesting day, which, when it was explained what he had in mind, was nothing short of the truth.

I walked up from the town, the sky still starry, and got to the house an hour early. I was familiar enough with its domestic arrangements to know that the servants would still be in their beds, it being winter. And if it should happen that old mother O'Gorman was up and stirring, she'd have to climb the stairs to catch me. She'd grown deaf over the years and now that the dog was buried in the orchard there was no one to alert her to footsteps. Even if she did rumble me, why, I could sweet talk her round in no time, and be given a bite of breakfast into the bargain. Consequently, I was easy in myself when I stole through the dark yard, past the stables and outhouses, and lifted the latch of the kitchen door. I took my boots off before I stepped inside.

It wasn't the first time I'd been in the house without anyone guessing. I did no harm, at least not of the lasting sort, and I didn't thieve. That would have been foolish and against my own interests. Nor did I ever venture above the ground floor. What I did on my dawn perambulations through the parlour, the dining room and the study was in the nature of an experiment. I moved things around – and waited to see who noticed. I'd begun in a small way, changing the poker from right to left in the grate, shifting a vase from the front to the back of the mantelshelf, altering the order of the musical boxes on the piano top. Then, after a few months, I became bolder and swapped the pictures from one wall to another. It took five weeks for Dr Potter to spot that the painting of ships in the river, previously situated behind the desk in the study, now hung beside the door.

The resulting rumpus, reported to me below stairs, was all I could have wished for. Potter repeatedly quizzed Mrs O'Gorman as to the character of the servants. She, good soul, swore they were all honest, and in their right minds besides, so he drummed up a notion about sleep-walkers and stayed up two nights on a chair in the hall, hoping to catch someone. Young Mrs Hardy, sickly again following another of her unsuccessful confinements, was kept in the dark on the matter. As for old Mrs Hardy, it didn't affect her in the slightest, she being uninterested in where anything was, as long as her bed stayed in its usual place.

Then, just as I was growing bored with the whole caper, mother O'Gorman let on that Beatrice Potter was convinced there were ghosts in the house and had even asked her husband to consult a clergyman. He'd refused and called her a fool, and there'd followed a shouting match in which Mrs Hardy added her pennyworth, informing Dr Potter he was the only fool she knew of and that she cursed the day Beatrice had ever married him. Later, Beatrice told Mrs O'Gorman she was worried it was the restless spirit of her dead father that was causing the mischief – which was the reason, this particular morning, for my being so early in the house. I intended to play one last joke.

I went first to the dining room. The curtains were still drawn and the room in darkness, but I knew it well enough to find what I wanted. Picking up the strip of Persian runner from beneath the windows, I crossed the hall to the study. The light of a gloomy dawn was already stealing though the glass, outlining the tiger's head where it nudged the fender beside the desk. Pulling the rug out through the door, I laid the runner in its place at the hearth, and then, keeping an eye on the stairs, began to drag the tiger behind me. I froze instantly, for the creature's claws screeched on the tiled floor and I was forced to hold it up by the paws and waltz it into the dining room.

I had intended to arrange it under the windows, where it used to lie when Mr Hardy was alive, only I was chuckling so much at the absurdity of my dance through the hall that I dropped it in a heap and helped myself to a mouthful of port wine from the decanter on the sideboard. Though some of it slopped to my jacket, most went to my head, after which it struck me it would be more of a jape if I draped the rug over a chair and had the beast's head pointing at the door. I drew back the curtains the better to see the effect. Beyond the windows the frosty orchard gleamed.

I was sitting at the kitchen table when Mrs O'Gorman rose from her bed. She made a fuss of me, which she always did, and seeing I had my boots off and was rubbing at my toes to get them warm, poked the fire into a blaze and put the kettle on the coals. I played up to her and let my teeth chatter, for I knew she had drink in the cupboard, having supplied her with it myself, and bought with my own money.

Not quite mine. Leastways, not at the start. It came from the proceeds of an investment provided by George Hardy some years past, to do with a woman whose memory he wanted stilled. He was a fool in the ways of the world, the woman in question being too addled with drink to remember anything longer than the immediate moment. I used the money to purchase a camera and the necessary chemicals, and once my enterprise was up and running I treated Mrs O'Gorman. She was an ignorant soul and I owed her nothing, but I hadn't a family of my own and it pleased me to buy her little extras.

Sure enough, when the kettle had steamed, she set before me a tumbler of brandy and hot water, to revive me, she said, and a slice of cold mutton to go with it. She wanted to know what Master Georgie needed me for at such a time in the morning.

'We're off to William Rimmer's uncle in Ince Woods,' I said. 'We're going to do something with an ape.'

She didn't hear me right away, and when I shouted louder and she understood, she screamed, 'An ape ... a wild beast?'

'Dreadful wild,' I hollered. 'It was transported yesterday from the Zoological Gardens in West Derby to Mr Blundell's place. Mr Hardy and Mr Rimmer are going to cut out its eyes.'

She grew quite pale and said she'd never heard of anything so horrible. That was a lie, or forgetfulness, for hadn't she suffered worse agonies of her own? Last Christmas, around the time young Mrs Hardy underwent her third miscarriage, she'd told me, weeping, that she herself when little more than a child had borne an infant by an older brother who'd buried it alive in a turf bog.

It took an age to get all the photographic apparatus loaded. Twice, we were half-way down the lane before George remembered something else that couldn't be left behind. We started off with myself at the reins of the carriage and he ahead on horseback, but for no good reason he changed his mind and took back the horse and climbed up with me: there wasn't room inside.

'Blazes,' he said, once we were on our way. 'It's infuriating the things one has to remember.'

'It is indeed,' I replied crisply, and bent my head against the wind.

I didn't wholeheartedly despise George Hardy, even though I considered him a hypocrite. He'd done me no harm, far from it, and I acknowledged his good qualities, including not being close-fisted. I dare say he could afford it, but often he treated broken bones and abscesses and the like, knowing full well his patients didn't have a button to their names. Hadn't he mended my mouth, damaged from my fire-eating days!

At the beginning, when chance had hurled us together, he'd offered me full-time employment, of a menial sort, in his household – blacking boots, seeing to the horses, running errands – but I told him straight I wasn't cut out to act the servant, not having the temperament to take orders. Some people find it comfortable to go through life on their knees, and good luck to them, but I prefer to keep my spine in the position nature intended. Besides, I already had my own means of keeping body and soul together, and after he'd learned me the tricks of the camera I earned a respectable living from the taking of shilling portraits.

I should have been grateful, but I wasn't, not entirely. What riled me was his lack of ease in my company, his keeping me at a distance, which couldn't be put down to differences of birth or education, for in his dealings with inferiors at the hospital his manner contained not the slightest degree of condescension or stiffness. With me, he held off. On the occasions when he addressed me directly I grew to fancy even his voice came out muffled, as though he spoke from within a nailed-up box. Since our first meeting he'd never once referred to that rainy afternoon when we'd carried a dead man across a field, but the recollection of it stood between us all the same, and when he looked at me I often thought he saw his father's hat jammed upon my head.

We took the Regent Road that ran beside the docks, the wind carrying the sickly sweet odour of damp grain, the air raucous with the screech of foraging gulls. We were forced to go at no more than a walk through the crush of vehicles juddering in either direction. Near the Brunswick Tavern a shipment of cattle, just then unloaded from Ireland and headed for the abattoir, came slithering and jostling across our path. George roared out, 'Whoa,' the command swooping out like a war-whoop, though it was me that gripped the reins. We were delayed for a quarter of an hour or more. He grew tetchy, fearful of missing his appointment with the ape, and vowed he'd never forgive William Rimmer if he commenced the business without him.

'What part am I to play?' I enquired.

'It will be your job to hold the animal down,' he answered.

I digested this with some unease. It was one thing to throw a tiger rug over a chair, quite another to subdue a wild beast.

'And it's then that you'll cut out its eyes?'

'Not out,' he cried. 'We shall merely remove its cataracts.'

I hadn't a notion of what these might be, and couldn't ask, for now he was on his feet, fairly jigging with impatience, rocking the two-wheeler alarmingly, kicking out at the nearest cow and shouting at the drover to make haste.

'Self-control is a great asset,' I observed, at which he shot me a look of fury, and sat down.

At Bank Hall, the dockyards coming to an end and the tide well out, we drove on to the shore, rolling beside the ink black waves, the sand hard as oak after the night frost. At a spanking pace we passed Miller's Castle, now empty, its forecourt silted up with mud, its bathing cubicles toppling into the mud pools.

'What news of Myrtle?' I asked, bellowing against the sea wind. Myrtle had been sent away to a boarding school in Southport. I'd seen her but once in two years, the time she'd come home for the Michaelmas holidays. She'd said she was glad the stain had gone from my lip.

'Miss Myrtle,' George corrected.

'Miss Myrtle indeed,' I said. 'I never doubted it.'

'She's on her way to becoming a lady,' he conceded.

'Does she take to it?'

'She blooms,' he replied. 'And excels in French.'

I had a photograph of Myrtle, though it was only me who would have known it. It had been taken in old Mr Hardy's bedroom and thrown aside on account of coming out black. I'd made pin holes in her eyes and scratched lines where her hair might have been, and in time I believed I saw her plain, though possibly she was in my head and it was my mind that printed her likeness.

At Little Crosby we left the shore, taking the cinder path through the sand dunes, until we reached the inland road and trotted a silent mile between potato fields. I had been brought up hereabouts, my mother being a drudge to a farming family in the hamlet of Sefton.

Crossing over the little humpbacked bridge, the rushes impaled in the frozen stream, we entered the leafless woods to a clamour of rooks. At the noise of our approach the lodge keeper hobbled out to see to the gates. He was so slow and crippled in his walk that George ordered me down to help him. No sooner had I done so and the great iron gates had swung inwards, than the carriage bowled up the drive, leaving me to follow on foot. I half thought of turning back, out of spite, but curiosity got the better of me.

I'd travelled this route once before, sent by my mother when she lay dying, only that time it was high spring. I was seven years old and there were pretty patches of heaven, lupin blue, dancing above the budding trees. Now, the path stretched dark and moody as a photograph, the winter branches stark against a cold white sky.

Blundell Hall was a gloomy edifice, low built of sandstone and timber. On either side of the porch crouched a stone lion with a man's head between its shoulders and a mocking smile to its mouth. I went round to the back and was told by a stable boy, just then unloosing the horse from the carriage shafts, that the gentlemen were in the glasshouse beyond the kitchen garden and I was to fetch the photographic apparatus along with me. When he saw the collection of bottles and trays that required shifting, he very civilly went off and brought back a wheelbarrow.

The glass-house was fully forty foot in length and no longer put to its original purpose, the long trestle tables being empty of pots and supporting instead a quantity of statues, all without a stitch on them and hung about with cobwebs. Mr Blundell was a collector of such things, and had been in the newspapers for it the year Prince Albert came to lay the foundation stone of the Sailors' Home.

The ape took me by surprise. I had expected it to be three times larger than myself and to find it wildly prowling its cage, but it was no bigger than a small man and sat inert against the bars, slumped amid a mess of sawdust and yellowing cabbage leaves. Fear left me; I even poked at it with my finger. Its skin was patchy, its eyes dull as mud. It stank of old age.

William Rimmer and George were busy sorting their instruments. Laid out alongside the scissors and punch-forceps sat a heap of cotton pads, a wire contraption with a coiled spring, an India-rubber bag with a length of tube looped into a metal basin, and a bottle of colourless liquid. The ape was looking past the table, in the direction of a marble statue with a severed leg. The statue was male, with a cock folded like a rose-bud.

'Ho, ho,' I cried. 'A Judy wouldn't find him of much use, would she? Even the monkey thinks so.'

'The ape is all but blind,' William Rimmer said.

George didn't say a word, which made it worse. I was angry with myself for appearing loutish.

A quarter of an hour later the latch of the cage was lifted and I stepped inside holding a pad saturated with ether. I took care to keep it at arm's length, being aware of its giddy properties. Ether was a component of the collodion solution painted on photographic plates, but mostly I used a commercial preparation from which the ether had evaporated while this was fresh from the bottle; already my eyes were smarting. The ape shuffled sideways but otherwise showed no sign of aggression. From behind, I clapped the pad over its muzzle. It gave an almighty start and rose off its shanks, flailing its arms and jerking its head backwards, catching me a crack on the forehead that nearly had me on the floor. 'Hang on, man,' cried William Rimmer, 'keep the pad in place,' and I did hang on, from fear of being trampled, though now I was damn near choking and mucus dripped from my nostrils. Like a man drowning, I fought against drawing breath, and just as I felt I could hold on no longer the beast shook me away, uttered a ghastly shriek, and scrabbling at its throat, fell down insensible. Piss steamed through the sawdust and splattered between the bars.

The three of us carried the patient to the table, securing its chest and forearms with straps. I was astonished at how closely the splayed limbs resembled those of a human, and one capable of arousing pity. Its head lolled sideways, exposing a patch of neck, hairless and wrinkled as worn leather. When the wire contraption was fixed to its skull and the spring prised up the lids of its eyes, I made to turn away, but Rimmer shouted, 'Stay where you are, damn you … put the bag over its nostrils,' at which George added, 'Please, Pompey,' and I liked him for it. It wasn't often he addressed me by name.

I scarcely saw what followed, for my eyes watered continually. I had the nous not to rub at them with my contaminated fingers, even though I was feeling uncommonly light in the head. The pulse in my neck thumped like a drum and I heard myself sniggering.

George wielded the scissors and Rimmer the forceps. They'd both wound strips of sheeting over the lower halves of their faces, which struck me as comical – likewise their conversation.

'Patient under,' intoned George, voice muffled.

'Shall I start?' asked Rimmer.

'I'm ready if you are – '

'I need to cough – '

'You can't – '

'Lens removed from right eye. Aperture stiff … Will need iridectomy.'

'Preparing to cut window,' said George.

My part, on request, was to pump the bulb supplying ether; not too much, for I'd been warned an excess could halt the poor beast's heart, nor too little, for then it might wake and its frantic thrashings cause the blades to snip too deep. In between administrations I was urged to keep an eye open for tremors and prod for rigidity of muscle, neither of which tasks I was in any fit state to perform, my breathing having become so laboured that each inhalation hurt like the devil. I was also nauseous and imagined I'd turned the colour of paper. For two pins I'd have left my post, only I doubted my legs would carry me.

The ungodly interference having come to an end, we returned the ape to its cage and I staggered outside. I retched, but my stomach was near empty and there was nothing to bring up save a watery fluid that stank of brandy. I had barely recovered when George ordered me back in again to put up the developing tent. No sooner had I shuffled away the dust and debris and erected the wigwam than he peered inside and pronounced it useless. It would, he said, admit far too much light. He was in the right of it; surrounded by glass we might as well have set up in the open air. He sent me off in search of a shed.

It took some time, most of the outbuildings being either piled with gardening and agricultural implements or else chock-full with broken statues too massive to shift. I came across a painted figure, shaped like a coffin and propped on end, its wooden casing rotted at the base. A lump of stained bandages poked out, nibbled by field-mice, from which three toes protruded, their bony segments the colour of honey. Then I thought I understood what had turned William Rimmer into a doctor, though for the life of me I couldn't work out what had influenced George, unless it was the sight of his mother's face looming above the cradle, eyes round as marbles.

It was the stable boy who showed me the ice-house, tunnelled beneath the rhododendrons and not twenty yards from the glass-house. George was satisfied with it, so I fetched the wheelbarrow and we got on with coating the plates.

The ape was awake on our return, and apparently none the worse for its torture. It sat with one hand gripping the bars, shaking its head from side to side as though baffled. William Rimmer, elated and sounding off like a preacher, declared that the veil had dropped from its eyes and it now saw the world clearly.

'Clever, what?' he crowed, thumping George on the shoulder.

'Damn clever,' agreed George, smirking with satisfaction.

I kept my opinions to myself; I didn't doubt their cleverness, but what use was a world only glimpsed from a cage?

When it came to be photographed the ape turned its back on the camera. First I tried shying pebbles at it, and when that didn't work, dragged the scissors along the bars. Its shoulders rippled, but it wouldn't budge. Then Rimmer hit on the idea of singing to it. He had a pleasant voice and warbled some kind of lullaby; sure enough, it did the trick, the beast swivelling round to stare at him. George took four studies, though the last was marred by the ape suddenly vomiting.

Once back in the ice-house, he developed the pictures by the puny gleam of a shaded candle, dipping each plate in a mixture of pyrogallic and acetic acid. It was my job, once George had judged the correct density of each image, to fix the results in a solution of potassium cyanide. Afterwards, he made me carry out the trays and pour the excess chemicals into the ground, on account of their being so poisonous. Often I'd washed my hands in the stuff to be rid of silver stains, and I reckoned he was over-cautious.

I ate my dinner along with the servants, and hardly did justice to it. My head ached and nothing tasted right. A footman ticked me off for coming to the table with blackened fingers. Too queasy to defend myself, I stayed silent. One of the women had been in service in Strawberry Fields and had known of Mrs Prescott and her daughters. She quizzed me as to Miss Annie's present condition and I said I believed she was in her fourth month and that this time she was holding. She said it was astounding, Miss Annie always being under the weather, considering she'd been so bonny as a child. I replied I didn't find it in the least astounding, and had known it happen the other way round.

'He's right,' agreed an old woman seated to my left. 'Look at our Henry,' and she pointed with her knife further down the table at a man built like an ox. 'Would you believe a breath of wind would have blown him away as a babby?'

The footman was curious to know what we'd been up to

with the ape; he'd helped manoeuvre the cage into the glass-house. After I'd enlightened him, he looked me up and down, scorn in his eyes, and remarked that he'd never have taken me for a doctor's assistant.

'I don't pretend to be,' I said. 'I'm a photographer.'

'Nor that,' he drawled. 'Though perhaps you come in useful when trundling a wheelbarrow.'

I rather lost my head, and spouted off about appearances not being everything, and how my father had been a gentleman and remained so, though in reduced circumstances. I could tell he didn't believe me, and was glad when he was summoned upstairs. My pa, so I'd been told, had enlisted in a Lancashire infantry regiment some months before I was born, and promptly embarked for India. To my knowledge, he'd never returned, either from choice or on account of colliding with his maker.

*

George sought me out in the late afternoon. It was obvious he'd had a fair amount to drink, for his speech was slurred. He said he'd decided to stay the night and that I was to return alone. Rimmer would lend him a horse in the morning. I was to stick to the main road going back, so as to avoid ruffians down on the shore. I knew it was his precious camera he was concerned about rather than my safety. I must be sure to tell his mother he was stopping over.

'Should my wife be unwell ...' he began, and hesitated.

'I'm to come back and fetch you,' I prompted.

'Perhaps ...' he dithered. His expression was anguished, his plump mouth drooping with discontent. He looked what he was, a spoilt man. Then, making up his mind, he blurted out, 'No, that won't be necessary. I shall be home before breakfast.'

I almost pitied him. For years he'd been at the beck and call of his mother; now he had a second woman to run him ragged. Mrs O'Gorman thought it a crying shame, but I reckoned he got satisfaction out of playing the martyr.

Ten minutes later, while I was in the yard stowing the apparatus, he sent out word that I was to wait for him after all. I've never known such a man for shilly-shallying. When at last he approached, leaning heavily on Rimmer, he insisted on clambering inside the carriage, where, scattering my carefully stacked baggage in all directions, he eventually burrowed himself into a corner beneath the folds of the developing tent. I reckoned he'd be asleep before we had quit the grounds.

The light was ebbing from the day when I rode away from the Hall. Once out of the trees I flicked the horse to a gallop, the carriage wheels lurching over the uneven ground, the wind swelling my clothes and blowing the ache from my head. Above the fields, black clouds tumbled through a sky white and glittery as ice. I had been melancholy on account of the footman putting me in my place, and angry with myself for having risen to his bait, but now the stormy landscape restored my spirits and I was seized with exhilaration. It did my heart good to think of George rattling insensible among the trays and bottles. 'One day,' I

shouted aloud, standing up in the traces like a charioteer,
'one day ...'

The tide was on the turn when I reached the sand dunes,
sashaying in over the waste of shore, the blood-red ball of
the sun dropping towards the horizon. Slowing the horse to
a reasonable trot I headed towards the gas-yellow haze of
the distant town.

Midway between Waterloo and Seaforth I came near an
old man before a driftwood fire, sparks whirling about his
head. I would have passed by, but just as we drew level a
furious banging came from within the carriage and I was
obliged to halt. George had woken.

If he was angry at finding himself on the sands he didn't
let on. Perhaps he was drawn by the picturesque aspect of
the scene – the bleak waste of dimming shore, the wind-
tossed blaze, the fiery snap and crackle of burning wood
above the hiss of the encroaching sea. At any rate, he asked
the old man if he could join him at the fire. He was, he said,
chilled to the bone, and indeed, in his flapping clothes he
appeared to tremble like a man in a fever.

The old cove didn't answer right away. I noticed he
glanced down to make sure the stout stick he used for
walking was within his grasp. Then he said George was
welcome, as long as he behaved himself, which tickled me.

He was talkative, and George treated him with politeness, addressing him as sir, which he'd never done for me,
though I expect it was the old man's years that made the
difference. I sat apart, watching the twilight dwindle and a
half-moon climb the sky. I thought of Myrtle, in her school-
room somewhere beyond the curve of the bay, spouting a

foreign language and learning to swoon when dogs barked too loud.

The old man had been a fisher of eels, so he claimed, for the pie trade in Widnes, until, some years past, fuddled in drink, he'd let his boat be smashed to pieces at high tide at Rock Ferry. His two eldest daughters had taken him in, or rather he'd divided his time between them, and gained little comfort from either. In that respect, George held, he was very like a king, which showed how tipsy he remained. The old man now lived with his youngest daughter in a lean-to next to a blacksmith's, and was at her mercy, which was why he slept nights on the sand. She had a mouth on her like a navvy and he preferred the nip of the sand-hoppers to the sting of her tongue.

'She's six young ones,' he said, by way of excuse. 'And no man to support her.'

'Life is cruel, sir,' George agreed, chucking another length of wood on to the fire, sending the sparks showering.

'If I had my chance again,' the old man said, 'I'd go for a soldier. They gives you a pension.'

'They also furnish you with a fair opportunity of getting killed,' George argued, at which the old man said there were worse ways of leaving this world than from the swift kiss of lead.

We left him then. A true philosopher, George called him, collapsing to his knees on his third attempt to climb up beside me. I bundled him inside the carriage, fearful he would do his addled self an injury and I'd be blamed for it. When I made to close the door, he seized my hand and tried to drag me in with him. I couldn't see his expression, for now it was night, yet his sly smile was imprinted in my head, mouth curved like those of the man-beasts keeping guard outside Blundell Hall.

I'd seen that face on him once before, after we'd laid his father down and Myrtle had been sent off to the kitchens to fetch water for washing. He'd thanked me for my help and declared I was remarkably practical for my age and that he would never forget my kindness, nor my reticence. It was my intelligence, he said, that rendered me incapable of taking advantage of the present situation. His words, spoken with such apparent sincerity of feeling, took me aback. Up until then I'd been biding my time, having every intention of squeezing five shillings out of him before I left the house. We were standing on either side of the bed, his dead father between us, and for one warm moment I did indeed imagine I was possessed of a superior sweetness of character. 'You're a good boy,' he murmured, and then he raised one knee on to the coverlet and hoisting himself up leaned across to touch my cheek. I knew instantly what he was about, and quit the room. I wasn't a stranger to that sort of happening, nor unduly alarmed by it, and if he'd not laid on the flattery I might have indulged him – it's not a vice restricted to any one class, though it's my experience that the better off bend to it from inclination and the poor more often out of necessity. It was his conning me into thinking I was something other than I was, something better, that shook me off guard. Dr Potter was coming out of the parlour as I ran down the stairs. Startled, I'd clung to the banister rail, expecting to be denounced. He'd never seen me before and he could have, should have, taken me for a thief, or at least demanded to know my business, but he just looked at me, and I fancied he read the trouble in my eyes. I had difficulty opening the front door; coming to my side, he tugged at the latch and let me out.

It was some minutes to seven by the Observatory clock when we crested the hill beyond the Boulevard and turned into Blackberry Lane. Within the carriage George was bawling at the top of his lungs the chorus of 'Mother Dear, I am Fading Fast'. The queer thing was, when we came to a standstill at the end of the drive and I helped him down on to the moonlit gravel, he uttered those self-same words of praise, *You're a good boy* – only this time, too late, I believe he meant it.

*

I brazened it out, of course, and think I got away with it, there being no evidence to incriminate me. It was Dr Potter who did the confronting, which was tricky, he being a man who saw through people.

He was waiting for George and beckoned him into the study the moment we stepped through the door. I went out to see to the unpacking, and as I came back in with the tripod and the tent, George burst from the room and ran ahead of me up the stairs. When I came down again Dr Potter was standing in the hall, staring at me. He said, 'Pompey Jones, I'd like a word with you when you've emptied the carriage.' I knew something was up from the look on his face; my stomach lurched. Each time I descended he was still there, still staring. Finally, I had nothing more to carry in and was about to lead the horse round to the yard when he came on to the porch and said I was to leave off what I was doing and come inside immediately.

I followed him into the study, heart thumping. I reckon it was the ether as much as apprehension. He took his time to come to the point, clearing his throat and fiddling with the buttons on his waistcoat. Most fat men look foolish when they're acting serious; not Dr Potter. I kept telling myself I hadn't done anything really bad, but his eyes made me believe I had.

At last, he said, 'I'm not unaware of the position you hold in this family ... and perhaps we are the ones most at blame. I'm not sure you've been given sufficient guidance – '

'I have received nothing but kindness,' I interrupted. I wasn't being insincere. With him, it wouldn't have been wise.

'That's as may be,' he said. 'You were little more than a boy when you came here ...' He paused, eyes searching my face. I put up my hand to cover my mouth, as though the mulberry stain on my lip had returned.

'But you are now a man,' he said, and again he paused.

'Yes,' I said. 'I believe I am.'

'A man,' he repeated. 'And a man must take responsibility for his actions, however innocently or ignorantly conceived.'

'It would be better if you came out with it,' I said, stung by his reference to ignorance.

So he enlightened me. First thing that morning young Mrs Hardy had gone into the dining room to fetch the needlework she'd left on the sideboard the night before.

'The curtains were still drawn,' he said, 'and in the half-light the rug appeared menacing – '

'The rug,' I blustered. 'What rug?'

'Frightened out of her wits,' he thundered, 'she turned to run out of the door and tripped – '

'Tripped – ' I echoed.

'She fell against the wall. Result ... a broken wrist. And that's not all ...'

I stayed dumb, but my face burned with shame. I truly felt remorse.

'A broken bone can be set,' he said. 'Dashed hopes are not so easily mended. You take my meaning?'

I didn't, not then, though I nodded.

'At first,' he went on, 'it was thought Lolly had been slovenly in her work. Mrs O'Gorman spoke up for her. She herself had inspected the room before she retired for the night and everything was in order. She said you were in the house at dawn.'

'I was told to come,' I protested. 'Master George told me to come. I know nothing about a rug.'

Mrs O'Gorman wept when I left the house. Half of it was on account of young Mrs Hardy having miscarried again, the other to losing me. She sniffed she wouldn't be able to bear it if she was stopped from knowing me. I told her she wasn't to worry, that things would blow over. 'George won't part with me for long,' I said. 'You'll see.'

I walked to my lodgings under a heaven sprinkled with stars. I wasn't cast down. One lives and learns, I reasoned.

Plate 3. 1854

TUG-OF-WAR BESIDE
THE SWEET WATERS
OF EUROPE

We began our ill-advised excursion to Constantinople on 27th February, sailing from Liverpool Docks on the Cunard steamer, *Cambria*. I speak of our expedition in such pessimistic terms, owing to the inclusion of the women and children, not to mention the maid and nursemaid deemed necessary to attend them. It had been originally planned that only George, Myrtle and I would make the journey. It could be, I felt, that in the advent of war, an event which day by day seemed more and more likely, George and I might be of use, he in his capacity as surgeon, myself as observer. Twenty years earlier I had visited the Crimea, in particular Balaclava and the coastal range, and, indeed, published a scientific paper at my own expense on the formation of the Steppe limestone common to the western portion of the Noghai plain. Result – no interest whatsoever, but perhaps that is beside the point. Myrtle was to accompany us for the simple reason that she was unable to let George out of her sight.

Quite when George had been inveigled into taking Annie along eludes me. There had been a cholera epidemic two years before, and fearful of another outbreak, she'd argued it would be safer for the children to be out of the town during the coming summer. No quarrel with that. I understood she had written to an aunt, who had a house overlooking the Menai Straits in Anglesey, asking to be allowed to stay there, and received a reply by return of post to the effect that she would be most welcome, and Beatrice too. As far as I knew, both women were perfectly content with the arrangement. Then, two weeks before we were due to depart, George feebly announced that Annie was coming with us after all. 'She insists on it, Potter,' he said. 'In the circumstances, how can I refuse? She is, after all, my wife.' I suspect Myrtle had a hand in it, on account of the children.

In vain did I lecture Annie on the intemperate climate, the frosty nights in early spring, the scorching months of July and August, the withering of the vegetation, the flies – she would have none of it. Optimistic fool that I was, I even gave her a book on the subject, which she took from me as though handling broken glass and deposited on the parlour mantelshelf, where it lay unopened. I have proof of that. Annie was addicted to crystallised almonds and Lolly spent her life sweeping sugar grains from the furniture. The marker I placed to indicate the relevant passages – the drying up of river beds, etc. – remained in an upright position and the pages pristine. Needless to say, once Annie was of the party, it became impossible to exclude Beatrice.

The *Cambria* was crowded, to the extent that we wallowed below the water line, there being two hundred troopers on board, four engineers, a veterinary surgeon and a representative of the Liverpool Board of Commerce, sent out to see what supplies might most be in need of urgent shipment should war commence. 'It is the patriotic duty of the citizens of Liverpool,' this gentleman informed me at the first opportunity, 'to make whatever sacrifices necessary in support of our army.' His name was Naughton and a more odious and obsequious individual could not be imagined. I had several heated conversations with him during the course of the voyage and formed the opinion that profit rather than patriotism ignited his sense of duty.

We were fortunate in the weather on the first leg of our journey to Malta, though one would never have known it from the groans and whimpers issuing from Beatrice. Nothing of note happened in the first three days, save for the ship's collie producing eight pups. Myrtle insisted on earmarking one, the runt of the litter, for the children. It would be good for them, she declared, to be responsible for something small and helpless. That same afternoon a so-called wife of one of the troopers gave birth to an infant daughter. Thankfully, it died three hours later, else Myrtle might have added it to our list of dependants.

The food on board was excellent. It would not be going too far to say we dined like kings. For breakfast there was pigeon, rump steak, cold hashed meat, eggs prepared in a variety of ways; hard-boiled, scrambled, coddled, fried. This feast was served up at eight o'clock sharp. Two of the engineers and, as bad luck would have it, the wretched Naughton generally kept me company. Neither George nor the womenfolk ever made it to the table. In George's case this was due to his having drunk too much the night before. Poor Beatrice, she who had boasted so loudly and so long of a desire to sail before the mast, had a miserable time of it, being confined to her berth, sick as a cat, except for those occasions on which Myrtle dragged her from below and marched her, distinctly green about the gills, up and down the deck. I could have been unkind – God knows, Beatrice has given me enough provocation – but I held my tongue. For all her faults, she had proved a satisfactory helpmate, particularly in regard to those intimate services required of a wife. Unlike Annie, Beatrice positively relishes her conjugal duties and has always brought a touching enthusiasm to her participation in our happy tumbles.

On our fourth day out it became apparent that Naughton was considerably smitten with Myrtle. She, as usual, appeared unaware of it, though she could scarcely move for tripping over him. It wasn't the first time she had caused a flutter in a manly breast, not that Naughton could by any stretch of the imagination be classified as manly. His lurch towards Myrtle surprised me. I wouldn't have thought he was discerning enough to appreciate her, he being the shallow sort of fellow susceptible to more obvious charms – a rosy complexion, sparkling eyes, splendid bust, etc. Myrtle was smallish, pale, had a chest as flat as a board, morose eyes of a colour neither green nor brown, and a somewhat sullen pout to her lips. It's true that when she engaged one in conversation, or was observed playing with the children, or she smiled, it was a different story. Then I do believe she cast a spell. Beatrice adored her, and Annie, who, God knows, had every reason in the world to find her detestable, showed signs of sincere devotion.

Naughton, struck all of a heap, went so far as to take George to one side and make his feelings known. 'Your sister is remarkably fetching,' is how he imprudently put it.

'I imagine that she has many admirers.' To which George rashly replied she had but one, to whom she was betrothed and who was waiting for her to join him in Constantinople.

I say rash, because it was highly likely we would continue to rub shoulders with Naughton when we reached our destination, and what did George intend to do then?

'Are you going to hire some young hussar to play the part of lover?' I asked him.

'I'll worry about it when we get there,' he retorted, and then drank so much during the afternoon that he quite forgot to tell Myrtle of her impending marriage.

Result – in the middle of dinner, the infatuated Naughton turned to her and blurted out for all to hear, 'Your fiancé is a fortunate man, Miss Hardy.'

The effect of this startling announcement on our section of the table was comical indeed. Annie, about to fork up a portion of pie-crust, sat with open mouth and implement suspended in the air. Poor Beatrice, already munching, choked on her morsel and might have expired if the veterinary surgeon hadn't thumped her between the shoulder blades. Myrtle alone stayed calm; gazing steadily at the speechless George, she replied, 'It's kind of you, Mr Naughton, but I assure you it is I who am fortunate.'

I don't know what she said to George afterwards. Nothing, I expect. George could do no wrong. If ever there was a woman with fairy dust in her eyes, it was she. Once, I had appealed to her to put a curb on George's drinking, which had grown excessive following the demise of his father. 'It's not for me to interfere,' she'd said. 'Besides, it makes him happy.'

Secretly, I wondered whether she didn't prefer him half-seas over: possibly it gave her more of a hold. He'd been shaken far more than was necessary at the circumstances surrounding his father's death. Though he didn't confide in me until some months later, I already had my suspicions that matters were other than they seemed. A relative of old Mrs Hardy, a Captain Tuckett, had come to the house the night it happened, and he'd told me that George was in a horrid state earlier in the evening, quivering and blubbing, and rambling on about Punch and Judy of all things. Then, of course, there was the sudden intrusion into the household of Pompey Jones – the duck-boy as Myrtle insisted on calling him – not to mention her own unexplained and astonishing elevation, packed off to boarding school as though she was a daughter of the family.

Myrtle was now indispensable. Old Mr Hardy had been a bully and a fraud, and as often happens with sons of such men – sensitive boys, that is – George had feared and admired him in equal proportions. It would not be incorrect to say that George had placed him on a pedestal, and a pretty lofty one at that. Mr Hardy's topple from the heights had shattered both of them. It was Myrtle's destiny in life to make George believe he had stuck himself together.

Several days later, when I was taking a turn about the deck, staring out at the monotonous vista of sea and sky, Naughton joined me and began a footling conversation on the construction of violins; the best wood, etc. He was a manufacturer of the things, with a thriving business, so he boasted, not a stone's throw from the Custom House. I am not a lover of music, though I once had the luck, during the celebrations surrounding the inauguration of the Albert Dock, to attend a piano recital enlivened by the soloist unexpectedly somersaulting from the platform.

Naughton was tedious enough when raving on about instruments, but he soon became even more so; he had the temerity to share his thoughts on the coming war. His ignorance of history was infuriating and his judgements worthless. It was his opinion that our affairs were *in the right hands*.

'By that,' I said, 'I presume you mean those buffoons who, by reasons solely of wealth and title, control both government and army?'

'Buffoons – ' he stuttered.

'Idiots, triflers,' I elaborated. 'No national respect for ancient tradition, no adulation of rank, however sincere, can fit an uneducated man for high office.'

'Uneducated?' he protested. 'Lord Aberdeen, the Duke of Newcastle, Lord Russell, Lord Raglan – '

'The want of educated men,' I thundered, 'has been the cause of our miseries in the East. They know next to nothing about the vast empire of the Turks. Our consular service, its members recruited from the aristocracy, live in their palaces as though the Thames flowed outside their windows. Their duties consist of home pursuits – the reviewing of parades, the throwing of garden parties, visits to the opera. They might just as well be living in Buckinghamshire. What reports have they sent on the nature of the climate, the terrain, the produce and resources of the country, the state of the roads?'

I was fairly shouting now. He looked affronted, which was gratifying. 'I suppose you have brought with you samples of building materials to show prospective buyers,' I continued. 'Brick ... stone, etc. There are, as you know, very few roads in the region.'

'I have not,' he said stiffly.

'Mark my words,' I said. 'There'll be a great call for bricks ... none at all for violins ... unless, perhaps, you intend Sebastopol to fall to the sounds of music.'

I had thought I'd put him in his place and he'd stalk off and leave me in peace. Not so; he stuck to my side like a burr. It's uncomfortable, being paced by a man one's insulted. Just as I was almost reduced to commenting on the waves and the clouds, their particular bounce and shade of colour, etc., he said, 'Dr Potter, what exactly is the situation of the young man Miss Hardy is to marry?'

'Situation ... ?'

'Position. What is his business?'

'War,' I said. 'He's a captain in the 11th Hussars.'

Then he did leave me, for who could compete with a peacock of the dazzling Light Brigade, however imaginary?

We sailed into Valletta harbour thirteen days on. Nothing would induce Beatrice to stay on board during the twenty-four hours required for the refuelling and restocking of the steamer. She was adamant that she must sleep on dry land, and failed to see the humour in my remark that, should she do so, she would find it somewhat strewn with boulders.

[74]

'There isn't a speck of soil on the whole island,' I informed her.

'Nonsense,' she said, pointing at the glowing fields above the harbour.

'Not *natural* soil,' I said. 'It was carted in from Sicily and elsewhere. The Knights of Malta allowed ships into the harbour only if they could pay their dues in grit and dirt.'

'What nonsense,' she said again. 'There is never any shortage of dirt, wherever one goes,' and she insisted I find her and Annie an hotel.

That afternoon our party wandered about the town, the women captivated by the jumble of peoples thronging the narrow thoroughfares. I found the place greatly altered since my visit two decades before. What, to a young man's eyes, had appeared an ancient stronghold, full of quaint architecture and exotically attired Arabs, Nubians and Jesuit priests, now presented itself as decidedly modern and raffish, the English influence being much in evidence. Time and again the women were forced to gather up their skirts to avoid the careless splatterings of the numerous red-coats who staggered out of the wine-shops and relieved themselves in the streets. I found this alteration disconcerting, and felt the burden of my years.

'When I first came here,' I told Beatrice, 'my hair was carroty –'

'I know it,' she replied. 'There were vestiges when we first met. The grey is a great improvement.'

We hired donkeys before dinner, plodding up the winding paths beside gardens splendid under foliage of date and palm, until we reached fields of barley winking gold in the sunlight. The children, lifted down, tottered round in the dust, swaying to the constant and pretty ringing of church bells floating up from the town. Their mother, safe from prying eyes, rained kisses on their baby cheeks and sang them nursery rhymes.

I spent the night in the hotel with Beatrice and Annie. It was a needless expense, but I don't sleep well without the warmth of Beatrice at my back.

We sailed the following morning, the talk at breakfast being that war was unavoidable. In two days' time no fewer than three French transports would enter the harbour *en route* for Gallipoli, their arrival to be greeted by a turn-out of the Guards and Rifle Brigade – this information from Naughton, who the night before had been up to the batteries for his supper. One of the engineers, whose word could be trusted, had confirmation that in our absence from England a siege train of eighty heavy guns had been assembled at Woolwich. Though to be expected, I found the news depressing; it is my belief that grim-grinning death is the only victor in war.

I passed the third night of our voyage to Constantinople on deck, having bullied a reluctant Beatrice to keep me company. She grudgingly admitted, when I tickled her from sleep at dawn, that a mattress and covers beneath the stars were in many ways preferable to the cramped confines of our cabin.

It was not a sudden longing to return to nature that caused me to shift us up-top, rather a desire to gaze once again upon the site of the hermit of Malea, a bearded solitary who, fifty years before, had built a shelter upon a promontory on the Cape, from which vantage point, cross-legged, he proceeded to contemplate the heave of the ocean. Twenty years ago it had been the practice of ships and yachts, after first blowing their whistles, to lower boats stocked with biscuits, salt and oil, and deposit such supplies, weather permitting, on the rocky outcrop below his dwelling.

'Legend has it,' I further informed Beatrice, 'that he came from Athens, where he was once a wealthy ship owner. Rather like yourself, his love of the sea' – here she flashed me one of her looks, of the sort guaranteed to turn a lesser man to jelly – 'was so great that he always commanded a ship of his fleet. On three occasions, the vessel he steered spun off course ... due to vagaries of the wind ... and foundered on the rocks off Cape Malea.'

'What rocks?' she said. 'I don't see any rocks.'

'They're out there somewhere,' I assured her. 'In despair, and to do penance for his drowned men, he vowed to retreat from the world.'

'Why the whistles?' she asked. 'If he does nothing but stare at the horizon, surely he can see the ships.'

'The word hermit,' I reproved, 'from the Latin *eremita*, defines a secluded place, a desert. He needs time to hide himself. A hermit cannot be forever hob-nobbing.'

'Well, he's certainly in retreat now,' observed my impatient wife, shivering at the rail and squinting out across the misty waters. Shortly after, she complained the salt spray stung her lips, and made to go below.

'Do stay,' I implored her. 'It gives me pleasure to have you stand at my side.'

[77]

'I won't,' she retorted crossly. 'I'm thinking of becoming a hermit,' and with that parting shot, she left me.

I never caught so much as a glimpse of land, though I stayed at my post for an hour or more, watching the racing sea and dwelling nostalgically on my long-gone bachelor days.

*

There are many things in this life capable of throwing people off course – the death of someone close, the loss of income or health, the realisation that cherished hopes cannot always be fulfilled. With regard to myself, nothing has affected me quite so brutally as that manifesto of the new sciences, *Principles of Geology* by Mr Lyell. I was twenty-two years old when I first read it. Result – I have not been the same man since. Echoing the sentiments of Mr Ruskin, I have often lamented to Beatrice, 'Those dreadful Hammers! I hear the clink of them through every cadence of the Bible verses.'

It was not so much Lyell's shattering of the fairy tale of Creation that plunged me into mental turmoil, rather his assertion that the interchange of land and sea is perpetual. Thus, our northern hemisphere, once a vast ocean sprinkled with islands, must, he argued, return to its original state, albeit in the remote future. It is not a comforting notion. Man himself is so buffeted by shifts of thought and mood, not knowing from one day to the next what he truly feels, that a shifting earth is well-nigh the last straw.

I was never more conscious of my tenuous hold on the

[78]

ground beneath my feet than during our first weeks in Constantinople, for nothing would satisfy the women other than to engage in a constant round of expeditions, luncheon parties and late night suppers. I exclude Myrtle, of course, who was diligent in taking the children to the sea-shore morning and afternoon, though this may not have been as good for them as she imagined. When we sailed into port it was Beatrice who noted the murkiness of the atmosphere. I was told that the Sultan had issued orders for all steamers to consume their own smoke – if true, its effect was negligible. 'One is reminded of Liverpool,' is how Beatrice put it, 'seen from the opposite side of the Mersey.'

It was astonishing how quickly the women adapted to their unusual surroundings. Conditions which would have had them in a faint at home produced no more than a reference to *quaintness*. Once it was established that the shrill humming which heralded each sunrise was not, as feared, the persistent whine of a giant mosquito but merely the muezzin's call to prayer, Beatrice was all for opening the windows, the better to take in the sound. 'How melodious,' she murmured, though indeed the reverse was the case. Even the hotel, which was no more than a large house, considerably deficient in comforts, drew no complaints.

It helped, I suppose, that we were all in the same boat, so to speak, for the town was swarming with English folk and we were never alone in our feverish activities. Casual acquaintances, of the sort who, in the sensible confines of our own country, would scarcely have rated a nod, leapt overnight into the category of bosom friend.

'He's surely a rogue,' I complained to George, when he

brought to our table in the Messieri Hotel a young man transparently disreputable. 'You would have shunned him at home.'

'We are not at home,' George countered. 'And I find him amusing.'

'She has a reputation,' I warned Beatrice, who, taking a lead from George, soon became on intimate terms with a Mrs Yardley, travelled out from England in the company of a colonel of the Guards. 'She is plainly connected to that gentleman without the benefit of marriage vows.' To which Beatrice tartly replied we were hardly in a position to throw the first stone. I confess she had me there.

The military news was confusing. On our arrival we had been told of a glorious Turkish victory and assured that the danger of conflict was past, only to learn the following day that the Duke of Cambridge and Lord Raglan were at this moment on their way to Malta to make a declaration of war. There were many among us, profiteers all, Mr Naughton being a choice example, who hoped the latter story was the truth. Meanwhile, we continued on our merry round.

Of all our numerous outings, the spectacle of the dancing dervishes remains most vividly in the mind, their performance being ridiculous in the extreme. It took place at Pera, in a small mosque adjacent to a harem. We were given seats in the gallery, from which we looked down on a circle of men garbed in long coats and wearing the sort of conical hats believed to be common to witches. In the centre sat a high priest, eyes closed as though he slept – and who could blame him? In the gallery opposite, a stout individual wearing a long beard and a silk dress decidedly feminine in design – Beatrice whispered she thought it divine – shook a tambourine and emitted a fierce howl whenever the fancy took him. For an hour or more we were subjected to a monotonous gabbling of prayers. Just as I was near swooning from boredom, the dervishes rose to their feet – they were immensely tall – cast off their outer garments and shoes and walked about, bowing ceremoniously to the priest and to each other. Then, at no apparent signal, they began spinning round and round. A more absurd sight could not be imagined, for they wore white petticoats and held their arms raised above their hats, so that they resembled huge revolving extinguishers. Efforts to suppress the hilarity raging through the gallery were far from successful.

Afterwards, Annie, Beatrice and Mrs Yardley gained admittance to the harem, where they were received by a Madame Kiasim whose raven locks were dyed buttercup yellow and who was reported to have read a French novel throughout. No other women were visible. A slave shortly brought in glasses of water and a plate of sweetmeats, Madame Kiasim later demanding payment for this refreshment without once looking up from her book.

In all this relentless gadding, this reckless bonhomie, I detected something of the hectic gaiety which must have prevailed during the last days of Rome. Like dervishes, we twirled from one diversion to another. At yet another picnic in the hills outside the town, the women's chatter rising like the twitterings of starlings, a premonition of impending disaster took such a strong hold of me that I was forced to leave the group and walk to a pinnacle some distance off. As I gazed below, to where the domes and slender minarets glittered amidst the cypress trees, a quotation came unbidden to my thoughts – *We have run this morning twenty-four miles, and could run forty-eight more. But who can run the race with death?* In the distance, beneath an azure sky, the narrow arms of the Bosphorus and Golden Horn, that perfect blending of land and water, pointed at the Black Sea.

That evening, when we returned to the hotel, we were met with two items of dreadful news; the first – depending on whether one considers things personal rather than universal to be of paramount importance – concerned Myrtle. In our absence the children had pined for a sight of their collie pup, housed down by the port. Sent for and let loose on the mosaic tiles of the forecourt, and no doubt terrified by reverberating footsteps, it had turned tail and lolloped back through the open doors, where it was immediately pounced upon by dogs, of which there are innumerable fierce packs roaming the streets, and torn to bloody shreds. Fortunately, the children, one toddling, the other in its nursemaid's arms, were too far behind to see the shocking assault.

Myrtle, in swift pursuit and coming in full view of the butchery, fainted clear away. Those who knew of her strength and singularity of character would have found her collapse hard to credit were it not for the testimony of the keeper of the hotel who had followed her abrupt departure from the premises. Restored, she had been helped from the scene of carnage by Mr Naughton and an unknown gentleman in military uniform.

The second piece of news, days out of date, was that England had declared war on Russia.

For a full week following this momentous announcement, we witnessed the most nauseating display of patriotic fervour. Cannons were fired by those ships of the fleet already returned to harbour after the supposed destruction of Sebastopol. The Messieri Hotel became a focal point for gatherings of English residents, all gesticulating like foreigners. It had seldom been safe to venture into the streets after dark, unless one cared to be jostled by drunken troopers, and now it became positively dangerous. Many a night we were woken by the gurgling screams of some poor wretch having his throat cut. Forced to stay indoors, we were subjected most evenings to the carollings of Mrs Yardley, who, accompanied at the piano by a haberdasher from Yorkshire, sang such sentimental ballads as 'The Soldier's Tear' and 'Yes, Let Me Like a Soldier Fall'. Mercifully, she appeared not to know that one time family favourite, 'Mother Dear, I am Fading Fast'.

George too was affected by the atmosphere, though he was touched by something more resonant than the trillings of the Messieri songbird. Before leaving for Constantinople he had sought an interview with the Army Medical Board in Manchester, and offered his services. In spite of possessing the right qualifications and having spent in excess of five years on the surgical wards of the Liverpool Infirmary, he was deemed unsuitable on account of his marital status. No objection was raised to his travelling out as a civilian, nor to his procuring a post for himself at the General Hospitals of Scutari or Gallipoli, but attachment to a regiment was out of the question. Since our arrival in the East he had made no attempt to make enquiries of either such place; when not on

the sea-shore with Myrtle, he had busied himself with pho-
tography or else disappeared into the Greek quarter of the
town with new-found friends. To be fair, he had practised
his trade when called upon, and without charge – treating
an elderly Greek lady for dropsy, dressing a burn on Mrs
Yardley's arm, lancing a child's boil, etc.

Now, he surprised me, for he lost no time in making
preparations to visit Scutari. His cause was helped by his
recent medical attentions to Mrs Yardley, her gentleman
friend, the colonel in the Guards, going out of his way to
assist him. It took longer than expected to arrange matters
and George fretted under the delay. Again he surprised me,
for he gave up his patronage of the Duke of Wellington
public house and scarcely wetted his lips at dinner. I found
this change of heart touching. He wrote long letters, many
to his mother, and even took the trouble to pen a few lines
to Mrs O'Gorman.

One evening, when we were sitting on the veranda of the
hotel watching the sun go down and waiting for the ladies
to join us, he turned to me and said he hoped I would
always be his friend. I replied indeed I heartily wished it so
– and he mine.

'You have always looked after me, Potter,' he said. 'And
I have not always taken your advice.'

'My dear boy – ' I began.

'I would like you to know that in the event of something
happening … something untoward … to me, that is, I have
appointed you my executor. I trust you're agreeable.'

'Come, come,' I said. 'What has brought this about?' I felt
uncomfortable.

As a man without resources – in terms of money – I have always relied heavily on George's generosity. It had been my dream that some bright day I might be able to repay him – through my writings; alas, it has remained a dream.

'Should I obtain a post at Scutari,' he said, 'it would give me great peace of mind if you would stay here and arrange passage home for Annie and the children.'

I agreed, of course. How could I refuse? He then began a rambling discourse to do with his past life, regrets, wasted opportunities, lack of application, etc., and how he felt, in some mysterious way, that the war would at last provide him with the prop he needed.

'Prop?' I said.

'Crutch, even,' he said. 'A man like me needs something to hold him upright. Beyond Myrtle, that is. There are things I have done that were *not right*.'

'In a hundred years,' I assured him, 'we shall all have forgotten the things that trouble us now.'

'I shall need a thousand years,' he said, and I swear he had tears in his eyes. His words made me uneasy; it is not generally a good sign when people like George lean towards introspection.

Just then Naughton came up and was no doubt taken aback at the warmth of my welcome. After much beating about the bush he asked George if the gentleman to whom his sister was betrothed had yet been called to active duty. George looked puzzled.

'Not yet,' I said. 'The rest of his regiment is still at Malta.'

'He's a good-looking fellow,' Naughton observed, in a distinctly wistful tone – at which it was my turn to be puzzled. Following some judicious probing I gathered he was referring to the soldier who had gallantly come to Myrtle's side during the shocking incident with the dogs.

'Are they to be married before or after the war?' Naughton asked, and it was then that George, irritated by such persistence, chose to break off Myrtle's engagement. 'He may be handsome, sir,' he replied, 'but he has treated my sister disgracefully. She will never be his.'

I remember how pleased we were at our inventiveness. It was, after all, nothing more than an amusing ending to a good, if rather cruel, joke.

*

It was decided that Beatrice, Annie and the children would sail home at the beginning of May, Constantinople having become insufferably crowded with troop transports and officials. Moreover, with the advancement of the season came an alarming increase in the number of flies and *things* that nipped in the night. It did no good to shake the bed linen from the balcony, as Beatrice took to doing morning and evening, for the verminous intruders were secreted in the floorboards and every slight crack in the walls. Annie, for one, couldn't wait to retire to the civilised surroundings of her aunt's house in Anglesey.

In April, George had achieved his goal, and now spent three days a week at Scutari, where he had been appointed assistant to a Turkish doctor at the Barrack Hospital. He could have returned each night, Scutari being no great distance, but felt it prudent to consolidate his position. His cases, as yet, consisted for the most part of falls from horses, injuries sustained in inebriated brawls and fever occasioned by venereal disease. In these parts a soldier could get drunk for sixpence and syphilis for a shilling. He said it was just as well he was not required to perform more surgery, facilities being primitive in the extreme. He reckoned there was a rat for every patient admitted.

He was a changed man. Though he returned weary and in need of a bath, hair cloudy with dust and clothes stained, his blue eyes conveyed a candour and innocence of spirit missing since his youth. Myrtle rarely accompanied him, due to the impending departure of the children. In this she was content, her love for them being quite simply an extension of her love for him.

In deference to the wishes of Beatrice, a last outing was planned – an excursion to the Sweet Waters of Europe beside the Golden Horn, followed by an evening at the opera. My feelings can be imagined, yet I smiled, feigning enthusiasm. I loved my wife, and indeed, the thought of parting from her, for Lord knows how long a duration, filled me with sorrow. How was I to manage? I dwelt sentimentally on the habit she had of sometimes picking at the food on my plate, the fond way her stubby fingers rubbed at my insect bites in the small hours. Needless to say, attempts to put my thoughts into words were greeted with irritation. Yet, when she slept and I made to move from the circle of her hot little arms, her clasp only tightened.

The Sweet Waters of Europe, a resort popular with all the Turkish rank and fashion of Stamboul and Pera, lay a fast two hours' ride across country. We were to picnic in the grounds of the Palace belonging to the Sultan's brother, a man celebrated for the beauty of his cultivated gardens and the hundreds of peacocks that swayed up and down his avenues of roses. I say fast, but as the children's necks were in danger of being dislocated from the jogging of the ponies, our progress was necessarily more sedate. We started soon after dawn but by eight o'clock the sun was already high and Myrtle wielded her fly-whisk above those downy infant heads as though warding off eagles.

It was pretty countryside we passed through and if it had not been for the temperature – a well-built man is rendered almost to lard by a fierce sun – I would have found it a pleasant enough way to spend a morning. We were trailed and sometimes overtaken by Naughton, who rode rather well for a violin maker. He was accompanied by one of the engineers and a skinny man in a turban. Each time Naughton drew close, he called out a greeting and raised his hat. Of course, he only looked directly at Myrtle. 'He stalks you like a hunter,' Beatrice said. 'I don't know how you bear it.'

'You forget that I understand obsession,' said Myrtle. 'Besides, what harm does he do?'

As we approached our destination, winding our way past the rustic villas that lined the water's edge, a flight of storks rode the blue heavens. For a moment we saw them clear, then, piercing the glittering sunlight around the golden dome above us, they flashed from dazzling view.

The Palace was built on a wide plateau, its grounds planted with trees and flowering shrubs. Leaving our ponies, we climbed a flight of steps and entered by way of a tunnel fashioned out of some sort of exotic privet. A hundred men, so Annie said, were employed in its upkeep.

The gardens beyond were extensive, an artistic blend of lawns, rockeries and herbaceous borders. I myself have never been able to raise much interest in horticulture, and grew weary of Annie's constant exclamations of delight at this or that example of what she termed an *exquisite bloom*. I was far more taken by the little clearings among the trees, in whose shade lolled parties of fortunate ladies, their scarlet fingernails languidly fanning the air. How I longed to join them! Instead, spurred on by Beatrice, who was driven forwards by the distant sound of clapping and muted cheers, we toiled down an avenue of purple rhododendrons and came at last to an open space ringed by boisterous spectators.

Here, the navy was holding an athletic sports day, presided over by a French admiral who, judging from the uncomplimentary remarks of several English onlookers, should have been occupied with more urgent matters, namely the conflict brewing beyond the Bosphorus. I rather agreed, though later, having caught a glimpse of this gentleman coming out of the refreshment marquee, gloriously attired in cocked hat and braided coat and supported on either side by blue-coats, I altered my opinion of his usefulness. It was evident from his drooling mouth and tremulous gait, each step placed as though fearful of encountering quicksand, that his days were numbered.

Presently Beatrice became absurdly engrossed in sprinting and jumping; unable to stand upright any longer in the blistering heat, I found refuge under a Judas tree and, draping a handkerchief over my perspiring face, fell into a reverie. My thoughts, possibly because I was thirsty, centred on the writings of Homer, in particular those verses dealing with the death of Antinous, stabbed in the throat by Ulysses as he was about to drink from the golden goblet – hence the proverb, *There's many a slip twixt the cup and the lip* – when I was painfully disturbed by a kick on the ankle. Snatching the cloth from my eyes I was in time to see an elderly gentleman diving across my legs and sprawling to my side.

I have often thought that most things in life are ordained and that there is no such thing as chance. Galileo Galilei could not have deduced that the earth spun round the sun without the inventor of the telescope having been born in his lifetime, any more than Myrtle would now be in her present proximity to George without an outbreak of small-pox and a visit to a brothel. These two examples, of course, are in no way to be compared in importance, but they do point to an extraordinary fusing of time and place. In my case, I have been the unhappy victim of predestination in that anything I might have had an aptitude to study has already been worked over by minds greater than my own.

I mention all this because the ancient man now lying alongside me under the Judas tree was none other than Gustav Streicher, the director of the Archaeological Collection at Kertch, whom I had known twenty years before. After assurances that no bones had been broken, there followed one of those conversations peculiar to encounters between comparative youth – my hearing was certainly superior – and extreme old age. I wasn't even sure he knew who I was, though he appeared to remember the marble head of Apollo whose tinge of rouge on the cheeks I had once so admired, also the sarcophagus with its two gigantic figures astride its lid, their heads knocked off by marauding Turks. I told him I recalled his inspiring lecture on the latter subject.

'Barbarians,' he muttered. 'Barbarians to a man.'

'And are you still at Kertch?' I asked, to which he replied he held a courtesy post, with pension.

'You prefer to live there ... rather than England?'

'What is England?' he retorted. 'Where is England?' I took this as rhetorical and stayed silent. I noticed his eyes had closed and hoped he slept rather than swooned from the effects of his tumble. Just as I was about to enquire whether he was all right, he cried out with great vigour, 'It is sheer nonsense to transfer the wanderings of Ulysses to the Black Sea. He would surely have mentioned the Dardanelles and the Bosphorus if his travels had taken place to the west of the theatre of the Trojan War rather than the Pontus Euxinus to the north.'

'Yes, indeed,' I said, and added, 'I'm here on a modern journey. I intend to be an observer.'

'Of what?' he queried.

'Why, the war,' I said.

'What war?'

'The present one,' I replied, disconcerted by the question.

'I know of no war,' he declared. 'Troy has been sacked.'

We were interrupted by Beatrice, who rushed up with the news that George was about to take part in the long jump, an event open to all-comers.

I helped the old man to his feet and shook him by the

hand. 'I remember you with fondness,' I said, though it wasn't altogether the truth. I had not forgotten the mortifying occasion, after another of his lectures, when, questions having been invited from the floor, he had called me an ass and told me to sit down.

'Hurry,' Beatrice urged.

'I hope we will meet again,' I said, shaking him by the hand.

'I trust not, Mr Lyell,' he replied, which at least showed a flattering remembrance of my geological pursuits, however wide of the mark. 'My regards to your daughter.'

'Did he mean me?' Beatrice demanded to know.

'Who else?' I said, at which she glowed.

George didn't do spectacularly well in his competition. His brother Freddie, alas dead from inflammation of the brain, had been the sportsman of the family. All the same, when he sped across the ground and launched himself into the air, the sun transforming his leaping head into a helmet of gold, we roared ourselves hoarse.

An hour later, as Beatrice was chivvying us to leave, George insisted we must pose for a photograph. He had seen a man with a camera standing before a dark tent near one of the fountains. So we lined up, some of us rearranging ourselves in the small hope of minimising physical defects, Beatrice, under the guise of appearing reflective, propping her chin on her finger, Annie slipping off her shoes so as to come down in height. As for myself, I took up the elder child, careful to let its petticoats dangle upon my belly, at which it howled and George ordered me to give it to its mother, who was already clutching the younger infant to her breast. Behind us, a tug-of-war progressed, officers versus men, the pig-grunts of the participants punctuating the struggle.

We stood there a long time, motionless as statues, except for the children. 'Be still, my sweet babes,' Myrtle murmured, as they leapt like fish in her arms.

*

Our visit to the opera took place at a late hour, long after we had eaten dinner. The theatre was in Pera, in the European quarter of the town, next door to a grog-shop bursting with soldiers. There was such a caterwauling issuing from within, one might have thought they were performing an opera of their own.

I was cross with Beatrice for making me put on my best clothes, the interior of the theatre being nothing short of filthy. Fortunately, we had a box and were somewhat elevated from the squalor. Even so, though I kept it from Beatrice, I brushed two cockroaches from her seat before she sat down. The stench both from below and from the establishment next door, a mixture of frying onions, beer and something sweetly rotten, was unbearable and kept us constantly flapping our handkerchiefs before our noses. Along the edge of the stage, perilously close to the tattered velvet curtains, stood a line of burning oil lamps, some with missing cowls. I took the precaution of examining the narrow passageway behind our chairs, and threw into the street several articles of broken furniture, which, in the event of fire, would surely have hindered our escape.

Myrtle sat as though in a trance, oblivious to her sur-roundings. Tomorrow the children would leave for England, and her heart had hardened to ice at the prospect. Then, some moments before the interval, I heard a strange mewing sound, which instantly brought back memories of Mrs O'Gorman's kitchen and the cry of the stable cat prowl-ing the bucket in which its kittens lay drowned. Startled, I glanced at Myrtle, and saw her cheeks were wet.

It was the music, according to George, that had thawed her, though how such a modern composer as Verdi, all discords and jangles, had the power to move anyone to tears, unless from sheer irritation, was beyond my compre-hension. Beatrice put a consoling arm round her, and Annie, who found it difficult to show sympathy, from embarrass-ment rather than feeling, ferreted out her smelling salts.

It was only after the curtain had fallen that I noticed Naughton in the box opposite, seated alongside his crony the engineer and Mrs Yardley and her colonel in the Guards. Naughton was staring to the left of our group, an expression of rage tormenting his features. Following the direction of his infuriated gaze, I leaned out to spy on the adjacent box. It housed an adolescent female, of dusky complexion, clasped in the passionate embrace of a young man brilliantly attired in the uniform of Lord Cardigan's 11th Hussars.

Some minutes later I saw Naughton making his way across the front of the auditorium. Arriving beneath our dusty cubicle, he looked up, first at Myrtle, who was in the act of dabbing at her eyes, then to her left. If such a thing is possible, I swear his lip curled. Then he walked purposefully towards the doors at the back of the theatre. Meanwhile, Mrs Yardley was energetically signalling to me, waving her programme and generally making a show of herself. As for the engineer, he was standing up, shoulders hunched like a prize-fighter, punching the air with his fists. I reckoned the pair of them were drunk and said as much to George, but when I succeeded in bringing his attention to the box opposite, the engineer had disappeared.

'It's extraordinary how foreign parts bring out the worst in people,' I remarked to Beatrice, who told me to shush as the orchestra were again filing into the pit.

The second half had just commenced, chorus gloomily wailing, when I heard footsteps thudding along the passageway behind. Then came a crash and a mumble of unintelligible words; my chair shook as something heavy bounced against our partition. Every eye in the house now turned in our direction, including those of the singers on stage. A voice – later identified as that of the engineer – distinctly shouted, 'Don't be a b— fool.' Craning forwards, I was flabbergasted to see Naughton, on his back, bent over the edge of the box next door at such an angle that his head dangled above the orchestra pit. He was leant over by the hussar, who had his hands round Naughton's throat. A good proportion of the audience, shamefully yelling encouragement, jumped to its feet.

There followed a most dramatic incident, far exceeding in authenticity and excitement anything we had yet seen on stage. Naughton, scrabbling desperately at his assailant's breast, managed to hook his fingers through the golden frogging of that splendid coat. The hussar, no doubt appalled at the thought of such defacement, loosened his hold and attempted to prise himself free, at which Naughton, levering himself upright and twisting sideways, jerked him off balance, sending him toppling across the edge of the box. Teetering, the hussar raised one hand, and tracing what appeared to be the sign of the cross, dropped to the boards below. For the first time I grasped the purpose of music, my emotions being considerably heightened by the continued playing of the orchestra – the unfortunate fellow landed to the accompaniment of percussion.

George hurried downstairs and, pushing aside the agitated crowd, did what he could for the fallen man. The rest of us stayed put, not wishing to add to the crush. There was a tremendous hubbub coming from the passageway; peeping out I was astonished to see Naughton being dragged off by half a dozen burly Turks. The engineer, much distressed, burst in among us and declared he himself was partly to blame. 'I should have stopped him earlier,' he shouted. 'By God, I could see which way the wind was blowing.'

Taking him out into the passage I asked him to explain what had happened. What was the quarrel about? Why had Naughton been attacked in such a brutal manner?

'It was Naughton who did the attacking,' cried the distraught engineer. 'He just dashed into the box and slapped the hussar across the face.'

'But for what reason?' I demanded, though I had a sudden and horrid suspicion I already knew.

'Why, on account of Miss Hardy ... for treating her so badly. There he sat, not ten paces away, his arm round that low woman ... and Miss Hardy in tears at the affront.'

'I advise you to go back to the hotel,' I said. 'In the morning ... when you're calmer ... we can call on the English consul.'

'I should have prevented him,' the engineer moaned, and ran off down the passage.

The affair ended better than one had feared. The captain, though bruised and having had all the breath knocked from his body, broke neither neck nor back. Suffering from nothing worse than a sprained ankle, he was helped to his barracks by comrades summoned from the grog-shop nearby.

George and I kept silent on the ride home. Both of us had reason to feel ashamed. I couldn't help thinking of the duck-boy, Pompey Jones, and how I had upbraided him over the childish nonsense of the tiger-skin rug.

Cause and effect, I thought. One should never underestimate the disruptive force of haphazard actions.

*

I rented the top half of a house at Scutari. George, who, until we joined him, had been sleeping at the hospital, was delighted at the move. Our windows overlooked the sea of Marmora and he was within walking distance, through the yard of a mosque, of the Great Barrack. Beyond what was absolutely essential, we had little in the way of furniture and Myrtle insisted it stayed that way. I was all for rushing off to procure sideboards and pictures and the like, but she said we weren't at home and it was no good pretending life was as it had always been. As it happened, we weren't destined to stay there very long.

A most remarkable change took place in Myrtle – in her appearance, that is. While George and I visibly lost weight, owing to heat and a restricted diet, etc., she appeared to gain some; her cheeks filled out and her throat and arms became rounded. Her face, once pale, turned golden in the sun and as she refused to cover her head, her hair leapt with threads of fiery colour. Result – it was as though Myrtle, previously lurking in mist, had now emerged into the light. I doubt if George noticed the difference, he being so preoccupied with other matters, but I did feel it was just as well poor, deluded Naughton was no longer on the scene. If he had been smitten before, this new, glowing Myrtle might well have sent him into madness. Naughton, after a hefty sum had been raised to sweeten the Turkish authorities – I myself, or rather George, having contributed generously to the fund – had been shipped off home. I accompanied him to the boat, where, before boarding and too distressed to speak, he clung to my hand like a drowning man. I'd adjusted my expression accordingly, though I reckon shame still swam in my eyes.

In June, George was summoned to Constantinople to appear before the Army Medical Staff. He was informed that henceforth he would be attached, in the capacity of Assistant Surgeon, to the 2nd division, presently to be quartered at Varna. He advised me not to tell Myrtle the reason for his appointment – no fewer than three doctors had successively held the post before him, and all had succumbed to cholera.

I expressed alarm, but he assured me that the danger of infection was as great here as there. For weeks, hundreds of the sick had been arriving at Scutari. The disease had taken such a hold that the dying lay in mouldering rows along the endless corridors of the Barrack Hospital. So much death and still a shot not fired!

I'm not a brave man and I must admit it did cross my mind that I might return to Constantinople and thence home. I suspect I would have done so, had it not been for Myrtle. Nothing on earth would have persuaded her to leave George, and if a mere woman was willing to stand her ground, how could I possibly turn tail?

We sailed a week later, in twilight, past the picturesque houses of the grand pashas; past the tomb of Barbarossa, conqueror of Algiers; past the darkening gardens amid the cypress trees, the keel of our ship trailing a dancing path of phosphorus light along the waters of the Bosphorus. In our wake flew a swarm of small birds, no bigger than robins, which are never seen to settle, but must always be in flight. The Turks, so I was told, suppose them to be the souls of women whom the Sultan has drowned.

Our journey took two days; on the morning of the second, while we were at table, a young officer in the Dragoons, in the middle of telling the company how he regretted leaving his tennis racquet at home, suddenly slumped over his plate. George, on propping him upright – he had attended him the night before on account of stomach pains – pronounced him dead. For a short while the dragoon sat there, mouth open. We too continued to sit, as though unwilling to interrupt him. When at last he was carried out, Myrtle rose and tenderly shook the breadcrumbs from his hair.

To say we landed at Varna was inaccurate; we fell down rather than disembarked, the pier being rotten. We had to wade through mud to reach solid ground. One of the horses broke a leg and had to be shot where it lay. It was dragged further out into the Black Sea, where it floated beneath a canopy of flies.

The town was in a state of considerable disorder due to its swollen population. The numbers of horses, troops and supply carts struggling up from the port made the narrow streets almost impossible to negotiate. There were rats openly burrowing among the mounds of refuse outside the provision shops. Even Myrtle remarked on the filth and confusion. My dreams of finding a pretty little house to rent, with tubs of plants on the veranda and the stem of a vine climbing to the roof, flew out of the window. Every available dwelling, beside providing refuge for numerous species of the insect world, was largely given over to human vermin, namely wine merchants and horse dealers, lured from every corner of the Levant by the heady stench of war.

George went off to report to the General Hospital, leaving Myrtle and me to wend our way some miles west of the town to where the army camp was stationed, tents pitched on either side of the road and extending upwards on to the hilly ground above a large lake formed by the river Devna. Downstream spread a second, smaller lake, the area surrounded by marshland which, though pleasant enough by day, at night gave off a noxious mist. I understood from the Greek villain who guided us there that it is in the vicinity of

[100]

the military burial ground in which lie the remains of six thousand Russian victims of the plague of '29. After purchasing, at exorbitant prices, tents and cooking pots, we settled ourselves some distance downhill from the smaller lake. As to drinking water, there were some excellent springs nearby.

It was only a matter of hours before I realised the extent of the dreadful pickle we were in; no sooner had night fallen than a wretched procession of men, some slung over the shoulders of comrades, stumbled past our fire and vanished into the darkness. I was told they were being marched to the river to clean themselves and were, as yet, suffering from nothing more serious than diarrhoea, although there were rumours that cholera had begun to rage through the French camp situated in the supposedly healthier region to the north-east.

George joined us a day later kitted out in what was claimed to be the uniform of an officer of the 2nd division. His garments were so faded and shrunken that it proved impossible to guess at their original colour; they had obviously been worn by the former unfortunate regimental incumbent – if not all three. Obliged, at his own expense, to purchase regulation boots, he was asked to fill out numerous documents, only to be told that it would be weeks, possibly months, before the desired footwear arrived.

Conditions at the hospital, he informed me, were disgraceful. There were too few sappers to put the place to rights and he gathered the authorities did not or would not recognise the urgency. Attempts had been made to improve the ventilation by removing planks in the roof, but the place was miserably dirty and provided a veritable Valhalla for fleas, cockroaches and rats. Nor were there sufficient medical supplies. On his first afternoon, he dealt with a man who, following a drunken fall from a horse, had broken his lower jaw. There being nothing else available in the way of splints he was forced to use the pasteboard covers of a book – *The Wide, Wide World* – to set the injury. Until whitewashed throughout the building remained uninhabitable, and it was his firm diagnosis that a man would die there quicker than in camp. He scratched ferociously all night long and robbed me of sleep.

I myself cut a sorry figure following the thoughtless handing over of the clothes I stood up in, much stiffened by my romp through the mud, to a washerwoman. Result – I spent a whole day, naked and wrapped in a grimy horse-blanket, waiting for her return. She never did, and to add to my sartorial troubles the ship that carried our trunks failed to arrive, having reportedly caught fire a mile out of Scutari. Myrtle went off and, finding a seller of second-hand clothing, kindly purchased on my behalf a clerical suit styled in a fashion last favoured by my grandfather. She also brought back a top hat, somewhat moth-eaten at the crown. I wore it, ridicule being preferable to sunstroke. She herself donned a long robe, such as worn by Turkish women, in which, almost indecently at ease, she glided about the camp.

It is curious how quickly one adapts to living in the open. Astonishing too, how used one becomes to hands black as pitch and a beard lively with grease. There is nothing more guaranteed to reduce a man to the essentials than to live beneath the sky.

I admit I didn't know who I was any more – my bearings had gone astray along with my trousers. I observed, and wrote down my impressions – by day, to the infernal buzzing of flies; by night, to the barking of dogs and the muffled cries of those disturbed by dreams of home ... and worse.

Deep down I was lost, my mind out of kilter. Often, drifting into sleep I silently recited those lines of Hesiod – *They by each others' hands inglorious fell, In horrid darkness plunged, the house of hell.* I fear it was the tough mutton we consumed at sunset, rather than intellect, that dictated my thoughts.

Plate 4. August 1854

CONCERT PARTY
AT VARNA

This is the most beautiful spot and I cannot understand why so many fall sick. Possibly it's the abundance of fruit to be had for the picking – cherries and strawberries grow wild in the meadows beyond the tents. I have never felt more healthy in my life.

On our arrival Georgie instructed Dr Potter to buy me a pony. She's white with a black patch on her rump; if startled, a blue vein stands out on her forehead. Docile animals are very like children. When I stroke her neck, the skin soft as velvet –

Georgie has never seen me ride, being always too busy, but yesterday he promised to come with me up into the hills above the lake. An hour before we were due to depart he went missing. He was in the hospital tent, of course, itemising medicines and jotting things down in a ledger. He has no assistant and complains of the amount of reports he has to submit to the office of the Inspector General. He could have said he was sad not to accompany me, but he didn't. He simply shouted over his shoulder, 'You go, Myrtle. I can't possibly get away.'

Dr Potter would have come with me if I'd let him, in spite of being an indifferent horseman and against exercise. I'm fond of him, but used to living mostly in his head he's poor company when forced outside. His frequent quotations concerning death, first spouted in a dead language and then laboriously translated, become wearisome. They're interesting as far as words go, and if we were sitting in a drawing room among fools I'd be the first to think him clever. Here, in the midst of the newly dead, his references to ancient massacres merely irritate. I suppose he scuttles into the past to escape the awful present.

'Mrs Yardley has agreed to ride with me,' I told him. 'And besides, you're not comfortable in the heat.'

'True, true,' he said, though he looked put out.

The sun being particularly fierce that morning, I begged to borrow his hat – to mollify him. Which it did. 'Take it, my dear girl,' he cried, tearing it from his head. I had no intention of wearing it longer than it took him to reach the shade of his tent.

Mrs Yardley and her colonel are billeted in the town, but spend their days in camp. I've grown to like her. Sometimes she swears, especially when newly bitten. She has several flea bites on her face, one on the end of her nose, yet remains good-humoured. She was on the stage, posing in operatic tableaux, and makes no secret of it, any more than she disguises the nature of her liaison with the colonel. I doubt she knows how much we have in common, although, owing to the incident with silly Mr Naughton, she has tried several times to sound me out in regard to background. As yet, I haven't taken her into my confidence, but may do so when I know her better.

We both do what we can in the way of relieving hardship

and agree that the wives and followers of the ordinary soldiers, some with children howling at their skirts, are more capable of fending for themselves than the 'ladies' among us. I keep telling Master ... keep telling Georgie ... that it's foolish to question the common soldier as to the looseness of his bowels, the condition being quite normal among those accustomed to eating food gone bad. I reminded him of Mrs O'Gorman's tale of her sister's family in Liverpool, who, finding the carcass of a long-drowned pig in the estuary mud, dragged it home and devoured it half raw. Result – as Dr Potter might say – full bellies for once.

Quite early on into our trek to the hills, Mrs Yardley began to probe; I reckon the colonel was behind it, he being acquainted with military gossip.

'Miss Hardy,' she said, 'I hear that Mr Naughton, on returning home, took to his bed. Apparently news of his exploits had run before him. He's now in financial trouble, due to neglect of his business.'

'I didn't know him very well,' I replied, 'but I'm sorry to hear it. Being without money is painful.'

'I thought you knew him in Liverpool,' she said.

'Not at all. We met on board ship ... and again in Constantinople. He was kind enough to help me back to the hotel after I'd turned faint in the street.'

'On account of the heat,' she said, still probing.

'Certainly not. It was the fault of the dogs – '

'Of course,' she cried. 'Beatrice told me. You were set upon – '

'I wasn't,' I said. 'A pet belonging to my ... my brother's

[109]

children was torn apart in front of me.' Just the mention of my darlings brought tears to my eyes.

'How distressing,' Mrs Yardley wailed, and sounded as if she meant it.

We skirted the river and passed a number of women washing clothes, their arms burnt brown from the sun. Close by, the Bulgarian provision men who supply the camp with meat were hacking at slaughtered sheep and flinging the bloody guts into the water. The women seemed happy enough, laughing and shouting as they rub-a-dub-dubbed. A small boy lay on his stomach, dipping a bucket. When full it was too heavy to heave out and he was forced to tip it sideways. After dashing some of the contents to his lips, he staggered off in the direction of the tents.

'I have never felt the need for children,' Mrs Yardley said. 'Which is just as well, seeing as I have never conceived.'

'Neither has Beatrice,' I confided. 'Though it's not for want of Dr Potter trying.' At which we both smirked, it being a risqué remark and one I would never have made to a woman other than my companion.

Thinking of such intimate things filled my head with pictures – Georgie fetching me from school in Southport and my seizing of his hand on the journey home – Georgie escorting Annie to a supper party in a hotel down by the docks, myself trailing behind, the early moon above, the lanterns lit in the rigging of the ships and my breast so full of innocent joy that I bit my lip for fear I squealed aloud. Not quite innocent –

'Damnation,' shouted Mrs Yardley, slapping her hand furiously against her throat.

I advised her to cut a cross in the nip, with her fingernail. Georgie says it disperses the irritation. Insects don't bother with me. Possibly I was so infested as a child that I'm now immune.

Soon the path led directly through a wood sweet with bird-song and the drone of bees. Mrs Yardley said it reminded her of being in church, without the inconvenience of having to kneel down –

It was at Mr Hardy's funeral that I was first in a church with Master ... with Georgie ... albeit in the opposite aisle and twelve rows behind. Lolly lent me her hat. Mrs Hardy sat between Beatrice and the gentleman who'd been shot at by Lord Cardigan. Nobody heaved with tears save for Georgie, although I admit I watched no other shoulders but his. Mrs Hardy carried a handkerchief and never used it. Some people only weep inside, which I think wasteful –

'Why do they find me so delectable?' complained Mrs Yardley, flapping her hands as the gnats swarmed about her head.

We rode in single file and shortly passed two young men, bare-chested in the sun-dappled shade, one sitting with his back to the trunk of a tree, the other sprawled upon the ground, arms covering his face, bright hair bunched against the brown earth. Both were lazily humming, their scarlet jackets dangling from the branches above. Hearing the soft plodding of the horses' hooves, the seated man opened his eyes and nodded respectfully; he had the rosy cheeks and snub nose of a country boy, and his lap was heaped with wild cherries.

Once out of the wood we began to climb higher. Mrs

Yardley, scratching at her cheek, asked what I would rather be doing at this moment in time. From her disgruntled tone it was obvious she had suddenly thought of a million superior ways of filling the hours.

'Why, just this,' I replied. 'One should always seize the present ... there is nothing else available.' I wasn't being truthful; I would have wished Georgie at my side.

Presently the path widened and we saw in the distance a little whitewashed house beside a square of vineyard. I was all for making a detour to avoid coming too close. 'There'll be dogs,' I warned. Mrs Yardley didn't appear to have heard me and trotted on regardless.

Sure enough, we had advanced but a little way when the air was shattered by a deep and awesome howl; Mrs Yardley's horse stopped dead in its tracks. An animal the size of a small calf and much emaciated appeared round the side of the house and tore towards us, followed by a smaller creature, black all over and running on three legs.

'Don't move,' I called out to Mrs Yardley, though indeed, the slither of claws on the stony path and the ferocious barking that rent the luminous day had turned her to stone in the saddle. Fortunately the horses stood firm, being no doubt used to such alarms. Some six yards away, the dogs halted, tongues lolling. I concentrated on the larger of the two, forcing myself to gaze into its hateful eyes; whining, it lay down, ears flattened to its mean and bony skull. Mrs Yardley was whimpering, but not loudly enough to provoke an assault.

After what seemed like hours a bow-legged man emerged from the vineyard and whistled off the brutes.

[112]

Approaching, he beckoned us forward. We were led past the house to a courtyard beyond, where a woman squatted in the dust pummelling a lump of dough. Fawning, the man urged us to dismount and gestured towards a rickety table. Half a dozen children, some crawling, materialised as though by magic and began to pluck at our clothes.

Mrs Yardley was trembling; a pin-prick of blood stood out on her cheek.

'Forgive me,' she said. 'I should have listened to you.'

'Think of what to give them,' I urged. 'Have you money?'

'Money,' she said. 'Why do we need money?'

'In return for hospitality,' I said, vexed. 'Nothing is for free in this world.'

The man set before us two small bowls and a pitcher of milk. The children got under his feet and he kicked out, scattering them squawking and fluttering, chicken-like, into the corners of the yard.

'Pig,' I exclaimed, though I was careful to smile. I thought it was no wonder the smaller dog had a leg missing.

Mrs Yardley was staring down at the jug, at the insects floating atop the milk. 'You must drink it,' I told her. 'If you don't they'll only bring us something worse.'

'At least they're past biting,' she said and gamely drank.

The woman slapped the circle of dough on to a flat stone; she pointed at the sun, then patted her stomach, indicating the bread would be good to eat when baked. As she lifted her arm her gown fell back and there was an infant stuck to her breast, scalp springing with hair the colour of tar.

'Think,' I urged Mrs Yardley. 'Think what we can give

them.' I myself had nothing, save a handkerchief at my wrist, mislaid by Georgie; she, a silk scarf at her throat.

All at once a curious giggling sound came from somewhere close to the vineyard wall. The bow-legged man swaggered off, and shortly returned carrying a struggling goat which he dropped on to its feet on the table. The children surged forward.

'If he's going to cut its throat in front of us,' Mrs Yardley promised, 'I shall scream.'

The goat had an aristocratic head and golden eyes; its front legs quivered. The woman left her baking and ran to stand beside it. Uttering one querulous bleat, the goat gave birth. Mrs Yardley jerked back in shock, a frill of milk edging her open mouth. Raking the amniotic slime from the kid's head, the woman blew into its nostrils, then gathered it up in her arms. A tiny fist poked from her bodice and waved beside a cloven hoof. Crossing the yard the woman flopped the infant goat down in the sun, alongside the rising bread.

Mrs Yardley offered up her scarf. She said the colonel had bought it for her, but it was worth parting with just to get away. She was no longer trembling and appeared quite recovered from her scare with the dogs. I reckon birth lifts the spirits, however lowly the species, life being so portentous.

We rode for an hour or more, climbing steadily towards the high ridge of trees that spread in a blue fuzz against the pale tent of the sky. According to Mrs Yardley, a huge bird circled above us and she wondered if it was an eagle. I couldn't help her; city bred, the only bird I knew of for sure was a pigeon. Besides, I was near blind in the dazzle of the sun and regretted not bringing Dr Potter's hat.

'Harry is very fond of birds,' Mrs Yardley said, speaking of her colonel. 'He shoots them in Norfolk.'

She wanted to talk about him, and did so, at length. She had met him five years before, in the street where her dressmaker lived. He had raised his hat as she passed, and when she turned round to look after him he too had turned to watch her go. 'Then, a week later,' she said, 'I met him again, at tea in the house of a friend. Hardly a word passed between us, but when we looked at one another our hands shook ...' She broke off and shot me a sidelong glance out of blue and vacant eyes – to judge if I was receptive.

'How romantic,' I said, obligingly.

'He escorted me home. We didn't touch ... not then. We just gazed ... then he called on me the next morning and simply said, "This was meant to be," and so it began.'

I remained silent, unable to think of a sufficiently suitable response. I didn't believe her for one moment – I mean, about their not touching that first afternoon. Women always want such things to sound less hasty than they generally are; I suppose it's because hesitation makes fornication seem less sinful.

'I find him middling handsome,' she went on. 'I like his chestnut hair and the set of his chin. Of course, you've noticed his beard, which is the colour of honey – '

'Of course – '

'As for the shine in his hazel eyes ... one can't fail to notice the twinkle.'

'I fear I'm short-sighted,' I said.

Beyond his looks, Mrs Yardley appreciated the way he treated her as an equal, except in matters of physical endurance. 'We are after all,' she opined, 'weaker than men and it's no use pretending otherwise.'

'Some men,' I corrected.

'We talk for hours at a stretch. I am never bored by his conversation. That's unusual, isn't it?'

'Very,' I said. Dr Potter holds that speech was invented to conceal thought, but I kept that to myself. Georgie's not one for talking, at least, not to me. Nor would I wish to be his equal, for then I might find him wanting.

Last week the colonel had celebrated his fortieth birthday. They'd dined in the best hotel in Varna. Poor Harry had drunk a little too much wine and his manservant had to help him on to his horse –

Fearing she was referring too much to herself – my expression was possibly not as animated as she would have wished – she asked if I was to have a birthday in the near future.

'No,' I said. 'I'm not even sure how old I am. Nineteen, perhaps ... but the date is unknown.'

'Good heavens,' she exclaimed. 'Why ever not?'

'My past is shrouded in mystery.'

'Good heavens,' she said again, and fell silent.

We had brought with us bread and fruit, and, arriving on the summit of the hills and refreshed by the faintest whisper of a breeze, dismounted and sat on the grass. Below lay the curve of Galata Point, the tents of the 3rd division, small as butterfly wings, quivering beneath the angle of the cliffs. A squad of toy soldiers drilled up and down before the glossy sea. William Rimmer is rumoured to be encamped at the Point, though as yet he and Georgie haven't met. Whenever he visited the house in Blackberry Lane he looked straight through me, and he kept Georgie up all night. Mrs O'Gorman used to whip me to be rid of passion, but it hasn't worked. I detested William Rimmer and still do.

'I don't mean to pry,' Mrs Yardley said, though indeed she did, 'but in repose you often look sad. Is it to do with your past ... or that business at Constantinople?'

'Neither,' I told her. 'I have a sad face. It's the way I am on the outside. Inside, I assure you I'm quite happy.' I was beginning to find her tedious, and pretended to doze off in the sun.

We rode back, giving the house by the vineyard a wide berth. It took longer, but Mrs Yardley vowed she would rather ride through a swamp riddled with snakes than confront again those hounds of hell. 'That baby,' she shuddered, 'with hair like the quills of a porcupine. That new-born goat sleek with scum ... that milk tasting of rancid cheese – '

We came at last to the trail that led into the woods above the lake. It was now past midday and we quickened our pace so as to be out of the glare. Ahead, the scarlet jackets blazed amid the leaves. A single beam of sunlight pierced the branches, framing in shimmering silver the outline of a man standing in the middle of the path. As we drew nearer he made no attempt to step out of our way and we were forced to rein in the horses. He stood with arms wrapped about himself, as though he was cold, and stared past us. Following the direction of his petrified gaze, I swivelled in the saddle and looked behind. The country boy still sat with his back to the tree, only now the pink had quite gone from his cheeks and his skin was mottled, like meat lain too long on the slab. He hadn't eaten all the cherries; flies crawled along his fingers and buzzed at his mouth.

There's a sameness about death that makes the emotions stiffen – which is for the best, else one would be uselessly crying the day long. It's why Georgie often seems insensitive to other people's feelings. Dealing with the dying, one must either blunt the senses or go mad.

The soldier wouldn't come with us, or speak. He and the dead boy stared at each other. We told him we'd send someone back to help carry the body down to the camp. He didn't seem to hear, just stood there, hugging himself. Mrs Yardley jerked the jackets from the trees and covered that purple face from view. It made no difference; the birds kept on singing and the men went on staring.

Mrs Yardley wept as we continued on our way. I was thinking of a fable I'd read about a monk who every evening heard the song of a nightingale. He asked permission to go and find the bird, but the Abbot said it was not for man to listen so closely to the voice of God. One night the monk crept from his cell, entered the forest and listened for an hour to the glorious outpouring of melody. He returned to find fifty years had passed in his absence and there remained but one member of the order alive to recognise him, the rest lying buried beneath the swaying poplar trees. I considered telling Mrs Yardley the story, to take her out of herself, but suddenly grew confused as to its meaning. Was it joy that had made the years fly, or was the monk being punished for disobedience?

When we came out of the woods I was weeping too, for I had pushed out the monk and fitted myself into the fable, and fifty years had passed since we'd set off that morning. I looked below, at the glitter of the lake and the spread of white tents, and dwelt on how bitter life would be if someone other than Georgie was left to remember me. Then I thought of him old, his hair grown white and me still a girl, and all that love I'd given him rotting like the cherries on the dead soldier's lap.

*

Two mornings ago Dr Potter heard that a concert party, made up of men from a rifle brigade quartered in the region of Galata Point, was to visit the camp. It was thought that it would boost morale, the cholera having now seized such a hold and still no date given for departure to the Crimea. Quite what might be offered by way of entertainment wasn't known, though rumour had spread that two soldiers of the line, previously belonging to a circus troupe in Paris, would be among the performers. Expectations were raised by the hammering into the ground of two stout poles some distance from each other, a length of wire strung taut between the two.

That evening, having received news of the forthcoming diversion, several French officers invaded the camp and caused Dr Potter inconvenience. According to him, he was fast asleep when the fastenings of his tent were wildly shaken. Rising from his mattress, Dr Potter asked what the commotion was about. He received no sensible reply, beyond being told to hurry up and that he shouldn't take all night. Puzzled, he emerged into the field, at which the intruders rushed inside without so much as a by your leave, and began turfing his belongings out into the darkness. Someone, either by mistake or from mischief, had told the officers that the tent did duty as a brothel. Dr Potter, still in his night-shirt, demanded an apology, and received none. This considerably upset him, as he has always held the French to be more civilised in their manners than the English. To make matters worse, one of the officers attempted to kiss him.

I spent the following morning helping to look after the orphaned children, of which there are now twenty or so, five being hardly more than babies. Of this number, half are genuine orphans, both parents having died, the rest unacknowledged by their fathers and abandoned by their mothers. Arrangements are in hand to have them taken back to England, but as yet transportation is not available. I don't find it easy to be with them, and would rather be doing different work. It's hard to love other people's children, particularly such scrawny and ill-featured ones as these. Fortunately, they are chiefly in the care of a good woman, wife of a sergeant, who has recently lost both her offspring from fever. I marvel at her fortitude. She tells me she feels tenderness through pretending the unfortunates are her own, and that I should do the same. She means well, and I hide from her how my heart leaps with terror at the thought.

In the afternoon one of the little ones crawled too near the fire and burnt its hand. I took it to Georgie, but the moment I entered the hospital tent he waved me away. He was with Dr Hall, principal medical officer of the expeditionary force, who had ridden out from Varna. The sergeant's wife plastered the child's hand with mutton fat, and rocked it to sleep.

When Georgie emerged, he looked subdued. He said Dr Hall was a tyrant and didn't know how to deal with people. He wanted too much done, too quickly. Nine men had died in the night, two only an hour before the medical officer's arrival, and he hadn't had time to write up the necessary reports. Dr Hall had called him incompetent in front of the men. He'd also flown into a terrible bate because most of the orderlies were drunk. He'd said it was up to Georgie to disabuse them of the notion that drink would ward off the cholera.

Dr Potter said that Georgie should stand up for himself and not allow the likes of Dr Hall to brow-beat him. 'You should have protested,' he argued.

'I did,' Georgie said. 'But he shouted me down.'

'It's disgraceful,' spluttered Dr Potter. 'You do the work of ten men.'

Then Georgie, being the way he is, abruptly did an about turn and said Hall was doing the work of twenty men and that he wouldn't have his job for all the tea in China. Later, he respectfully escorted his superior as far as the dirt road beyond the camp.

When he returned, Dr Potter suggested he should rest for an hour. At first Georgie said it was out of the question, though he'd been up all night and could scarce keep his eyes open. When he relented, I made to go into the tent with him, but he pushed me away, muttering he must be left alone. I reckon it was because I had my menstrual flow. He has a sensitive stomach for that sort of thing, in spite of being a doctor and used to blood. Five minutes later Dr Potter joined him, and I could hear the murmur of their voices. I do understand that Georgie prefers the companionship of his own sex, men being so afraid of women, but sometimes I almost wish he'd fall sick, so that I could look after him.

The concert party entered the camp in daylight, marching behind a bullock cart piled high with musical instruments and a quantity of painted scenery. I was at the spring washing clothes when they passed. We have a servant, of sorts, a Greek boy hired by Georgie in Scutari, who is meant to do such tasks, but he is believed to have a woman in another part of the camp and often goes missing. Dr Potter says he ought to be got rid of; Georgie, soft-hearted as always, won't hear of it. I don't mind doing the washing; it gives me pleasure to swill the dirt from Georgie's shirt.

That evening he insisted we took dinner together, which was his way of saying he was sorry for his earlier brusqueness. He doesn't usually relish eating with me, on account of my failure to disguise appetite. The boarding school I was sent to taught me the right cutlery to use, yet failed to instil what he calls the correct attitude to the table. At home, if I'm invited out with him and Annie he insists I eat before we go, as I haven't the knack of picking at food, possibly because I went so short of it in earlier days. Here, thankfully, we have

[122]

only one dish and a spoon, and are required to devour everything very fast, otherwise the flies settle on it.

Mrs Yardley and her colonel 'dined' with us, as they were staying on to attend the concert. They were obliged to bring their own food, our cooking pot being on the small side and our rations rather low. The provision men don't come to the camp as often as they once did, on account of the sickness.

The colonel insisted on sitting beside me, which was annoying as he has a nervous habit of jerking his knee against whoever is placed next to him. He and Georgie discussed what Dr Hall, in the middle of his bullying, had referred to as the infernal muddle of the war. The initial object of the campaign – to prevent the Russians taking Constantinople – having already been accomplished by the unaided efforts of the Turks, he'd heard it was proposed to lay siege to Sebastopol.

'We have to do something,' argued the colonel. 'We can hardly turn tail and go home, not after all the flag waving and drum beating.'

'But when?' demanded Georgie. 'This year, next year ... when?' In Dr Hall's opinion the delay was a direct result of the ditherings of the government and the conflict raging within the High Command, neither authority having anything other than the vaguest notion as to the possible strength of the Russian forces. The decision on when to make a move had been shifted on to the shoulders of Lord Raglan, now housed in a cockroach-infested villa in Varna, mind rocking under the realisation that his supplies were wholly inadequate and his army decimated by disease.

'He has only one hand in the muddle,' announced the colonel. 'He lost the other at Waterloo, along with his arm.'

'Cockroaches,' shuddered Mrs Yardley. 'Now he'll know what the rest of us endure.'

'I speak confidentially,' Georgie said. 'But I was given to understand by Hall that over eight hundred men have perished this month. He recommends our own immediate removal to higher ground.'

'Where the French are,' said the colonel. 'And they too are dying.'

'*Dulce bellum inexpertis*,' put in Dr Potter. Mrs Yardley promptly nodded earnestly, as though she understood, which stopped Dr Potter from his usual helpful translation and left two of us in the dark.

The entertainment commenced an hour later. Dr Potter declined to come with us, thinking the word concert implied a diet of music. A makeshift stage, consisting of ammunition boxes, had been constructed close to the lower lake. It was illuminated by a row of lanterns hung along the wire stretched between the previously erected poles, thus dashing the hopes of those anticipating the thrills of a tight-rope act.

The scenery was both ingenious and artistic, being composed of a folding screen painted on either side, the one depicting the interior of a railway carriage with a window cut in it, the reverse showing a splendid portrait of Queen Victoria with a lion at her feet.

The concert began with a novel rendering of 'She Wore a Wreath of Roses', the 'she' of the title, simpering within the railway carriage, represented by a stout soldier dressed in female clothing and wearing on his head an absurd circlet of vine leaves, the grapes dangling about his ears. A second soldier stood in the frame of the window and sang to the plucking of a banjo. Out in the darkness a tambourine jangled.

The laughter and cheering that accompanied the first and second verse was enthusiastic enough, but when it came to the last –

> *And once again I see that brow,*
> *No bridal wreath was there ...*

(here the banjo player snatched away the coronet of grapes and planted a pair of women's drawers in its place)

> *The widow's sombre cap conceals*
> *Her once luxuriant hair;*
> *She weeps in silent solitude*

– the words were entirely drowned in the merriment of all concerned. So great was the hubbub that the songsters were obliged to enact it all over again, with the audience joining in the chorus, though the words were different. When I asked Mrs Yardley about this she said the army had their own version and didn't I think the original lent itself to *double entendre*.

This so puzzled and occupied me – I wondered whether the women's drawers gave a clue – that I scarcely took notice of the next two items on the programme, one of which was a military song and the other a juggling act, the latter performer being booed off the stage and his skittles thrown after him. This cruel response was possibly due to the circumstances in which we find ourselves; far from home and stalked by death, there is a need to be heard.

The ballad that followed had a curious and wondrous effect on Georgie. It was called 'Saved by a Child' and was very suspect, about a man grown tired of being bound to the earth and earthly things, sitting in a church watching a child. The man couldn't bring himself to pray, on account of being world weary, until the child's singing began to melt his sophisticated heart.

Half-way through this sentimental verbiage, Georgie reached for my hand. He doesn't drink any more, so I was startled. I didn't respond, not right away, in case I put him off. He whispered, 'Myrtle, dear Myrtle, forgive me.'

'For what?' I asked.

'For everything,' he said. 'I give you so little time.'

'Your work is important, Georgie.'

'That's no excuse,' he said, and added, 'I'll come to you later.'

Then I pressed his hand, out of love, not forgiveness.

In the interval, mad with happiness, I ran to fetch Dr Potter from his solitude. He was searching himself for lice by the light of a candle. Impressed by my gaiety, he shook his clothes into place and agreed to join the party. Georgie shifted his seat to afford him room, leaving me squashed against the colonel who was drinking wine from the bottle. His knee jerked worse than ever, but what did I care?

We were a quarter of the way through the second half – Dr Potter was slapping his stout thighs with delight and carelessly swigging the colonel's wine – when the fire-eater came on. He was dressed in a spectacular tunic of scale armour embroidered on the breast with a green dragon belching flame. Underneath he wore tights, and some bright sparks shouted out they admired his legs. With his wig of black ringlets and the rouge on his cheeks, he could have passed for a girl, and a handsome one at that, if it hadn't been for his moustache, which was curled up into two stiff points. He was featured within the railway carriage, where he set ablaze a length of tow placed on a plate before him. 'Pardon me,' he called out, 'while I partake of a light supper,' and forking the burning stub into his mouth, puffed out fire. He did this twice, and chewed the tow all up, or, at least, we never saw him spit any out. He did the same with some sealing wax, and bits of scarlet dripped to his chin and went on burning, which was more satisfactory. Then an assistant came on carrying a bag labelled gunpowder and proceeded to help him off with his tunic and wig. He had dark hair underneath and a pale smooth body. The gunpowder was genuine enough; an officer, picked at random, was hauled up to confirm its authenticity.

The fire-eater hunched his shoulders, poked his head forward, tortoise fashion, and stretching his arms out sideways stood as though prepared to carry our Lord's Cross. In each fist he clenched what was pronounced to be an onion. The assistant, taking his time, opened the bag, made a show of peering inside, and shuddered. The fire-eater hollered out that he was feeling the chill and urged him to hurry. A heap of powder was poured into the hollow between his shoulders, then, like a farmer sowing seeds, his accomplice trailed the blue-grey dust the length of those spread arms. Finally, he turned the fire-eater round so that his back was to us. A lighted taper was handed through the cut-out window. The assistant took it, held it aloft for all to see, and slowly brought it down.

The audience had gone quiet – you could hear the frogs croaking in the reeds beside the lake. I peeped to look at Georgie. He was craning forward, frowning.

As the gunpowder flashed, the crowd jerked in shock; a fuzz of blue flame sizzled along each arm as far as the fire-eater's fists; smoke curled out of his uncurling fingers and tatters of burnt onion dropped to the stage. He didn't appear to have hurt himself, though he kept his hands held up when he took his bow, like children do when their palms have been whipped.

The colonel said it was a damn dangerous thing to try, and there was no trickery in it. He was lucky not to have had an arm blown off. Had the fellow lost his nerve and lifted his head by a fraction, his hair would have caught fire. I turned to gauge what Georgie made of it, but he wasn't there. I asked Mrs Yardley if she had seen him and she said he'd rushed off thinking he recognised someone.

The concert party finale thrilled us all. The troupe, minus the fire-eater and the juggler, and swelled by a dozen or more soldiers of the Rifle Brigade, clambered up on to the boards and stood to attention while they lustily sang of death in battle. Dr Potter blew his nose violently, a sure sign he was moved, which was unusual bearing in mind his aversion to melody. It was the boy bugler's plaintive accompaniment to the twice-repeated line, *Enough they murmur o'er my grave, He like a soldier fell*, that stirred the heartstrings most.

How strange it was to be encamped in a foreign land, Queen Victoria plumply gazing into the mist-wreathed night, the voices ringing out beneath the hidden stars! How portentous the message, how wrapped in sentiment the cheapness of life!

Dr Potter thanked me for forcing him to be there. He said it was good for men to weep. He and Mrs Yardley swayed as they walked. We tripped over two figures on the ground, one still moaning, the other cold. The colonel strode off to alert the stretcher bearers, but when they came they were staggering in drink. 'At night all cats are grey,' quoted Dr Potter, and clung to Mrs Yardley for support.

I left them as soon as politeness allowed. Once in the tent I cleaned myself as best I could, wiping my armpits and other, more secret places. Then I extinguished the lantern light and waited. Georgie is coming, I whispered.

I fancied I could smell onions, though it may have been the memory of the fire-eater's act that haunted my nose.

I waited a long time. The human noises died away and the frogs croaked again. Sometimes I floated off and walked through a garden in Cheshire, belly swollen, fingers snipping off blown roses. I could hear the clack of Annie's knitting needles. Once, Mrs Hardy hovered above me, demanding to know what I'd done with the tiger-skin rug. A pearl of mercury slid down my eyes, but it was only a diamond of light shining through a hole in the canvas.

When at last I rose and emerged into the open, the mist was rolling away across the lake and dawn streaked the sky.

Not a yard distant a man and a woman lay on their backs in the dew, she with her legs splayed wide. They were sleeping, not dead, for their mouths gaped open and both were snoring. A dog had its snout in Dr Potter's cooking pot tipped from the fire.

Georgie was in the medical tent, fast asleep on a straw mattress behind the instrument table. His arm was flung out across the chest of the fire-eater, who, covered in a hospital night-shirt, the rouge still hectic on his cheeks, lay on the bare ground beside him. This close, I knew him; it was the duck-boy. He had a blister on his lip and blobs of sealing wax spattered his beard.

Behind me a sick man called out for water. He was trying to raise his head, the claw of his hand raking the air. I took no notice and slipped away. He swore after me.

When reveille sounded I found myself at the lake, though I have no recollection of walking there. By now the crimson flush above the hills had faded into shining day. I stood, resentment wriggling like a worm within my breast. It had been my conceit that it was enough to give love, that to receive it would have altered the nature of my obsession. When passion is mutual, there is always the danger of the fire burning to ashes. Rather than lose love it was better never to have known it.

A crane sailed down the sky and landed in the reeds. It frightened me that the child who had trailed Master Georgie at a distance was now treading on his heels, clamouring to be noticed. I knew I was in the wrong; Georgie had made no promises, raised no false hopes, and yet … and yet –

A voice called out, 'My dear, what a night. Wasn't it

amusing?' and Mrs Yardley, her hair spilling from its pins and her face creased, waded through the grass. The crane splashed upwards. Then, remembering the sick soldier craving water, misery overflowed and I wept.

Mrs Yardley was very sympathetic. I was in a state to behave stupidly and went half-way to confiding in her. I admitted, or rather hoarsely sobbed, that I loved Georgie. Just voicing it gave comfort.

'Of course you do,' she soothed, and patted my hand. 'It's only natural.'

'Last night, after the concert, he said he'd come to me – '

'Come to you,' she repeated.

'But he didn't – '

'He has his medical duties,' she said.

'What about his duty to me?' I cried. 'What about me?'

'There, there,' she murmured, 'you poor child,' and took me in her arms, which dried up my tears, for there's nothing I dislike more than to be pitied. I'm not a 'poor' child and never was, unless the description is strictly related to poverty. It was on the tip of my tongue to tell her that Georgie owed me something, on account of the babies, when she said, 'I wish I had a brother,' and that closed my mouth. I'd forgotten she supposed I was Georgie's sister.

When I returned Dr Potter had rekindled the fire and put the water on to boil. He was attempting to grind coffee beans with the heel of his boot.

'Pompey Jones is in the camp,' he said, stomping away. 'He and George have gone to the river to wash.'

'That time Mrs Yardley and I were frightened by the

dogs,' I said, 'I saw how they dealt with the beans. They had a crusher with a handle.'

'Well, I haven't,' he retorted, and stamped the harder.

I changed my dress for the duck-boy, not Georgie. He was taller than I remembered and fuller in the face. His black hair, damp from his swim in the river, was drying into curls. He strode right up and took my hand, saying he was heartily glad to see me. He wasn't at all shy or subservient. It had been three years since last we met, at Christmas, the time I'd come back from being made into a lady and gone to Georgie's room in moonlight.

*

The concert troupe posed for a photograph before marching off. Preparing the plates for the camera proved difficult because flies kept sticking to the collodion mixture. The duck-boy wasn't a soldier but an assistant to a photographer he'd met in Chester who thought the world of him. They had been sent out by an important newspaper. He had taken part in the concert at the last moment, owing to a colour sergeant who recited monologues succumbing to the fever. Before leaving England he'd gone to see Mrs O'Gorman; she'd cried at the sight of him. He'd found her in good health apart from a certain stiffness of the joints, which was only to be expected at her age.

Georgie helped with the photographs, even though it meant neglecting his medical duties. The results would be sent back to England, so that the public would be aware of the good times the troops were enjoying. Dr Potter said it was a case of securing the shadow ere the substance faded, meaning, he gloomily prophesied, that it was likely those captured by the camera would shortly be dead.

Georgie was allowed inside the photographer's van. It was a curious vehicle, painted all over in white, its sides slotted with glass windows. When disembarking at Varna it had nearly sunk in the mud.

The duck-boy and Georgie spent most of the morning discussing thicknesses of solution, physical as opposed to chemical development, the effects of temperature and the exactitude necessary for exposures. Georgie's own equipment had been lost when the ship caught fire out of Scutari, and Dr Potter declared messing about with Pompey Jones would do him more good than a week of rest.

Later, I encountered Mrs Yardley. She was saddling her horse, and crying. At first she said she didn't want to talk about it, then almost immediately did so. She had spied the colonel twinkling at the wife of a captain in the Grenadier Guards. I thought her foolish for letting on she'd noticed. It would have been wise to turn the other cheek.

The performers departed at midday, leaving the duck-boy behind. He was his own man as regards time. He sought me out in the afternoon; I was in the open, cutting Dr Potter's hair.

'Well, Myrtle,' he said. 'Was it worth it?'

I replied I didn't understand the question.

'Being turned into a lady. Is it what you expected?' He was eyeing me steadily, from head to foot, taking in my faded gown and the men's boots I wore; they were practical because they stopped the insects fastening on my ankles.

'I don't regret it,' I said, defensively. 'If that's what you mean.'

'From what I hear,' he said, 'you've been done no favours.'

Dr Potter jerked his head from the scissors and said, 'I note you're as insolent as ever, Pompey Jones.'

'That's observant of you,' he retorted. 'But then, I was never made into a gentleman, was I?' He fingered his blistered lip. 'I shan't do the fire-eating again,' he announced. 'I've lost the knack.'

'Certain knacks are better lost,' remarked Dr Potter. They stared each other out; the duck-boy's lashes were singed. Brushing the hairs from the shoulders of his stained coat, the doctor retreated down the avenue of bell tents.

'You shouldn't speak to him like that,' I said. 'He's an educated man.'

'He understands me,' said the duck-boy. 'He always did, and not on account of his learning. For what it's worth, I reckon him and me see eye to eye.'

He was digging into the pocket of his vest as he spoke. 'I've something to show you,' he said, bringing out a flat object wrapped in the folds of a red handkerchief. Uncovering it, he held out a square of copper plate. It was black all over with some scratch marks in the middle.

'What is it?' I asked.

'Why you, of course ... standing by Mr Hardy's bed.'

I was astonished to think of him keeping the picture by him all these years, particularly when there was nothing to see.

'Today is in the nature of an anniversary,' he went on. 'It was August, if I'm not mistaken, when I first saw you – '

'In that house,' I said. 'On the stairs with the broken banister – '

'Before that … you were sitting on the station steps … in the rain … in Lime Street.'

'You did a good thing,' I told him. 'A boy stole the woman's duck and you brought it back.'

He laughed at me then, and explained it was nothing but a street trick. The station was a good place to try it on, what with the waiting and the dumped down baggage. They worked in pairs and split the money. One boy did the thieving and the other the retrieving. Even if the owner didn't cotton on to what had been lost, ten to one a passer-by with more bobsticks than sense, noting the return of property, would hand over a few coppers – as a reward for honesty. Sometimes the accomplice said, 'No, sir, I cannot profit from doing what is right,' and more often than not the amount was doubled.

I was speechless.

'Of course,' he said, 'you had to know which ones were gullible, otherwise you might end up with nothing more useful than the promise of a corner in heaven.'

Deep down I thought it a clever trick, though I declared he should have been ashamed of himself.

'I never was,' he answered, voice flat, and asked if I was content with my life.

I nodded.

'I know about the children,' he said. 'From George.'

At this, I felt elation, because it meant that Georgie had

bothered to talk about me. The lingering resentment at his preferring to be with the duck-boy dropped clear away, and suddenly the day was beautiful, the vista of tents and distant lakes, previously grey under a leaden sky, now miraculously glowing with radiant light. A troop of horses trotted towards the dirt road, coats silky in the sunlight. I enquired what else Georgie had confided.

'Just that,' he replied. 'And that he was glad ... seeing that Annie was no longer capable of producing offspring.'

I might have accused him of being the cause of her disappointment, due to his shenanigans with the tiger's head, but then, hadn't I every reason to be grateful for the outcome? Instead, I blurted out, 'I love him. He is my reason for living.'

He looked at me sombrely and asked, 'Did they send you away, then?'

'Not on my own,' I protested. 'Both times Annie and I went to a cottage ... in the country. At night she knitted and I told her stories. I had to make them up in my head because she's allergic to books. I respect her. She has never shown jealousy.'

'Why should she?' he scoffed. 'She has never known hunger.'

He wouldn't stop questioning me. He wanted to know what old Mrs Hardy had thought of it all, and I said I didn't know, but that, like me, she'd only ever wanted Georgie's happiness.

He looked away. I fancied he was sad. Presently he murmured, 'I'm thankful I'm not a woman.'

At that moment Dr Potter returned, carrying a haunch of

mutton. Jubilantly he described finding a provision wagon overturned down by the lake. It was empty, but after searching about he'd come across the meat lying at the bottom of a slope.

'That was lucky,' said the duck-boy. 'Particularly if there was no sign of the driver.'

'Indeed there wasn't,' the doctor retorted crossly. 'Otherwise I should have paid him.' Sitting down on his stool, the leg of mutton clasped between his thighs, he began to pluck off the maggots. Soon after, the duck-boy left us.

'He knows about the babies,' I said.

'From Mrs O'Gorman, no doubt?'

'Georgie told him.'

'Then Georgie is a fool. One should never confide in the Pompey Joneses of this world.'

'What have you against him?' I asked. 'Georgie likes him, and thinks him kind, as I do.'

'Not so,' he said. 'He may yet do you both harm – '

'He keeps a picture of me,' I protested.

Then Dr Potter said that keeping the picture was an affectation, as was the apparent kindness. 'One day the mask will slip,' he warned. 'As Seneca succinctly put it, *Nemo potest personam diu ferre fictam.*'

I didn't wait for the translation and walked off. I wished it was Georgie who held my picture against his heart, however darkened by time.

Plate 5. October 1854

FUNERAL PROCESSION
SHADOWED BY
BEATRICE

I have taken to dreaming, and not only at night. In the past – what years have turned to dust in the space of eight weeks – it was the approach of darkness that brought on fantasies. Then, the image of Beatrice stayed within the cup of my shut eyes. Now, she zooms free, circling my head; I would take her for my guardian angel save that she frowns so. Only the other morning I was disturbed by George pumping my shoulder with his fist. He was shouting, 'Potter, stop it. Stop apologising.' I protested I hadn't spoken, but scarcely had the words left my mouth than my wife's face, distorted with irritation, loomed up in front of me. The wind was tugging at my clothes and blowing the smoke into my eyes, yet her glare held me captive. To cope with this visitation, for I am not yet mad, I reminded myself that a thirst assuaged by water pissed in by dying men and a stomach subjected to hunger were guaranteed to spore hallucinations.

We left Varna the second week in September, along with some sixty-four thousand British, French and Turkish soldiery. Many of the women were turned away from boarding, and rejected, stood wailing on shore. Myrtle, by virtue of her peasant dress and brown complexion, and leading her pony laden with baggage, was let by without hindrance. Mrs Yardley wasn't with us; she'd fallen out with her colonel of the roving eye and gone home. I was glad she could no longer fasten on to Myrtle. The two were incompatible, not least in their attitude to virtue, Mrs Yardley's conviction being that the easy sort was sinful.

George was wild with anger, owing to the compulsory leaving behind of a great deal of hospital equipment, including ambulance wagons, litters and operating tables. There simply wasn't room. He was all for going on shore to demand they be loaded, but was assured they would be sent out later.

We waited two days before sailing, during which time the sickness continued. At night the bodies were flung overboard and sank, the bubbles winking in the lantern light. By morning, the weights having worked free, the dead achieved a bloated resurrection and bobbed to greet the sun.

Once out at sea some said we made a splendid sight, the fleet arranged in five lines, each composed of a division of the army, the French on our right flank, the navy to the left, the Turks a little behind, Lord Raglan out in front. I didn't share the enthusiasm, the men about me presenting a sorry picture, their once fine uniforms much tattered and their boots worn through at the soles.

Worse, that first night fire broke out in the hold. Patent fuel had been mixed up with the coal and become heated. Result – spontaneous combustion. The smoke was dreadful and all were required to help shift the stores up on deck. Not until the hoses had extinguished the blaze did I learn that ninety tons of ball cartridges had been stored alongside the coal, without the protection of a magazine. Throwing the ammunition over the side had been deemed unthinkable, although the risk of blowing all on board to Kingdom Come was considerable.

We landed at Kalamita Bay, on the western shore of the Crimea, on the 14th of the month. No one knew whether the Russians had any knowledge of our coming and I was full of apprehension as to what awaited us. In the event, nothing did, nothing in the way of a human enemy. The beach was deserted and the ridge of distant hills bare of either troops or guns.

We camped further along the Bay, waiting for the cavalry and artillery to disembark. That night it rained, and it was not the gentle drizzle of an English autumn but a monstrous pounding that drowned the fires and churned the ground to mire. A few had tents, the rest put up blankets, but both means of shelter collapsed under the force of the downpour and one was drenched to the bone. My letter from Beatrice, received at the end of August and containing homely news – the weather was fine, the children well, the air of Anglesey conducive to a sharpening of the appetite – was blotted beyond recall. I tossed it into the mud; nowhere had it said she missed me.

Reveille sounded at 3 a.m. the next morning, and not many of the fit had to be shaken from slumber. We rose as we had horribly dozed, shivering in our clothes. There was no wood dry enough to make fires and we went without breakfast. My hat, formerly too large, had shrunk, and I was obliged to bind it to my head by means of a strap.

It took a further day and night, both fortunately fine,

before the supplies were unloaded, the sick taken back to the ships and the dead buried. George was dismayed to discover that not a single ambulance wagon had been brought ashore and precious few stretchers. Nor was there enough food, though later some Tartars arrived at the camp willing to sell sheep and a quantity of wine. This transaction had barely been completed – the cooks were engaged in slitting throats – when a pack of dogs rushed in, and, rounding up the living animals, cunningly scurried them away. Shots were fired after the retreating Tartars, but no one had the energy to go in pursuit.

In the morning a chaplain conducted divine service. Though I'm an unbeliever, the ragged voices singing familiar hymns brought water to my eyes. In the afternoon George was ordered to report to one of the steamships. He returned with the news that he had been relieved of his present post and was henceforth attached to the Royal North British Fusiliers, a Scottish regiment, his predecessor having fallen overboard midway between Malta and Gallipoli. He was togged out in the shrunken uniform of an officer of the 21st, and had inherited a blood-letting bowl, a leather apron, almost new, and a tin of leeches, the occupants long since expired. As the Fusiliers were not required to wear kilts, he supposed he should be grateful for small mercies.

At last, on about the 18th, the order came to march. We set off in great style, the band playing, spirits high. Anything that lay ahead was thought to be better than the hell of inaction we had recently quitted. Nor were the troops burdened with excessive baggage, each man carrying on

back or saddle nothing that couldn't be rolled up in a blanket. Hadn't he with him the only two things that mattered,
a stout heart and his weaponry! As long as the cavalry had
their swords and lances, the infantry their Minié rifles, the
artillery their howitzers, what else, on God's earth, was
needed! Inessentials such as tents, cooking pots, medicine
and changes of clothing would surely follow.

We marched all day. The band stopped playing after the
first hour. Once we had our backs to the sea the flies returned. We started without water and found none on the
way. Some of the sick got at the wine and it was the end of
them. They lay down at the wayside and slept into death. In
the beginning we tried to urge them onwards, talking to
them of home and mother and loved ones. Later, we
trudged by without a glance.

I had no horse, thinking it too much trouble, and regretted it. Myrtle plodded beside me. Exhausted as she became,
she wouldn't mount her beloved pony, convinced he carried enough weight. He was called Seel, after the street in
which she'd been found. She'd brought with her two or-
anges, one of which she used up squeezing between the lips
of a boy trumpeter. His last words were comical. He said,
'Good Lordy! Another day.' Myrtle wanted to keep the
remaining orange for George, but thankfully he had gone
on ahead. I swear it saved both our lives.

When I had the breath I told Myrtle about the little villages I had once visited in the vicinity; the grapes growing
on the vine, the black bread that could sustain a man for a
month. She chewed on orange peel and flicked the flies from
her face.

I dreamed again, of walking through the plum orchard in Blackberry Lane. Beatrice was on the swing, pushing her little white slippers against the air. I called, Be careful, not too high, and she called back, You were never one for the heights, and pushed the harder. I walked away, hoping to make her come after me, but she didn't.

'She was never afraid of losing him,' I said, and I must have been talking out loud because I heard Myrtle say, 'If you're referring to Annie, why should she have been? She never knew hunger.'

We covered twenty-five miles, over scrubland, and climbing higher bivouacked at dusk beside a small river. Nothing, I foolishly thought, not even Mardonius's advance across the plain of Plataea, could be compared to the brutality of that march.

*

It had been believed when we disembarked that the army would advance directly on Sebastopol. Bickering having broken out between Lord Raglan and the French – his Lordship favouring an attack from the north, where the fleet could give protection, the French preferring a thrust from the south – this design was not carried through. Result – we stayed put for several days and the Russians mustered reinforcements.

Finally, orders came through that Sebastopol was to be encircled. I have always liked the word circle, reminding one, as it does, of childish games, Pig-in-the-middle, Ring-a-ring-a-roses, etc. Dr Johnson gives it much space in his dictionary; a line continued till it ends where it began; an assembly surrounding a principal person; an inconclusion found in argument, in which the foregoing proposition is proved by the following, and the following is inferred from the foregoing. This latter definition appears to me to furnish an accurate description of the muddle of this war, though perhaps *tishoo, tishoo, we all fall down* is sweeter on the ear.

Yesterday, Myrtle's pony suffered an injury. We had ridden out to find fruit for George. Supplies having failed to arrive, our diet is severely restricted to salt beef and biscuits, and Myrtle was determined to venture into one of the villages. I could not help thinking that poor Naughton might have made himself a fortune if he had stayed on and applied himself to the grocery business.

Earlier, during the laboured encirclement of Sebastopol and our trudge to the Chersonese plateau, I had purchased an ill-tempered little mare for five pounds, there being, for obvious reasons, an abundance of animals without owners. I also managed to procure a greatcoat and a forage cap. I had no wish to accompany Myrtle, in spite of my warmer clothing, but felt it my duty.

The plateau on which we are camped is roughly the shape of the Isle of Wight, Balaclava lying to the east, Sebastopol to the south. A steep escarpment, the Sapouné Ridge, overlooks land between the Tchernaya River and Balaclava. We rode in an easterly direction and I cautioned Myrtle to go slowly as the path was littered with small stones slippery under the rain. She was singing, though how she could be so merry in such dismal circumstances passed my understanding.

We had been riding but half an hour when, mounting a ridge, we were afforded a glimpse of Balaclava, the masts of ships spread in a cat's cradle across the bleak sky. At that moment the mare stumbled, and, giving vent to temper, promptly sank her teeth into the flank of the pony, who, bucking with pain, shook Myrtle to the ground.

She cried out at once that she was unhurt, and got to her feet. I thought it strange that she didn't immediately see to the pony; instead, trembling violently, she pointed at the ground. There, not a few inches from where she had fallen, lay a human limb – a leg torn off a little above the knee, toes poking through the shreds of a cavalry boot.

'I was sold a melon in Balaclava,' I said. 'By an elderly woman on a mule.' It was the truth. I couldn't remember clearly what season it had been when first I visited the Greek fishing village on my tour of the coast, though I doubted it was winter, on account of the melon.

'The Tartar name for the place was Kadikoi,' I continued, 'meaning the judge's village.'

Myrtle showed no sign of interest, which was a pity because I had a host of relevant facts in my head.

The town of Balaclava is situated on an inlet running deep into the land. Behind lies a basin of dark waters, surrounded, with the exception of a narrow gorge, by precipitous rocks which rise to an elevation of a hundred feet. In my time the Greeks possessed their own court of judication, and an independent magistracy whose president was responsible to the Russian authorities.

While strolling beside the water I had noticed the presence of medusae, a sure indication that this was no lake but a gulf connected with the sea by some narrow outlet. The ascending slopes were not, as I had thought, formed of nummulite limestone but of Jura rock, pale red in colour and of a striking aspect at sunset. Numerous ruins stood on the summit, including the remains of a castle from which the entrance to the straits was commanded. I would have climbed up for a closer inspection had it not been for a weakness of breath, and instead returned to the village where I encountered the woman with the melon. Strolling about, the juice running down my beardless chin, I came to the opinion that a harbour more protected against storms and sudden attack would be difficult to find.

I had at that time about my person a copy of that passage in Homer's tenth book of the *Odyssey* in which he describes the approach to the country of the Laestrigones, lines which Pope admirably translated thus:

> *Within a long recess a bay there lies,*
> *Edged round with cliffs, high pointing to the skies;*
> *The jutting shores that swell on either side,*
> *Contract its mouth, and break the rushing tide.*
> *Our eager sailors seize the fair retreat,*
> *And bound within the port their crowded fleet …*

In mentioning this passage, I should not like to be accused of attempting to prove too much by means of too little: indeed, I am in full agreement with Professor Streicher of Kertch in thinking there is not a scrap of evidence to support the dubious theory that Ulysses entered the Black

Sea. All the same, it is remarkable to find a spot which so entirely blends with the poet's description of localities.

I speak, of course, of Balaclava's past. Alas, from what George has told me, its melon days are over. Now the headquarters of the British military forces, he has visited it twice in as many weeks in an effort to procure medical supplies and blankets. His description of the filth in the streets, of the harbour choked with the bloated carcasses of horses, camels and the occasional human, is disturbing. Our ships are loaded with provisions which, owing to bureaucracy, inefficiency and the difficulties of transportation, stay rotting in the holds. On the quayside, at the mercy of the rain and circled by starving dogs, lie hundreds of wounded waiting to be dispatched to the rat-infested wards of the hospital at Scutari.

In such circumstances, I presume death to be preferable to life. Strange to think that the dying, ignorant of history or art, feast dull eyes on a landscape, its dwarf cypresses scattered across the slopes, reminiscent of a painting by the sublime Titian.

'I wish to go back,' Myrtle said, turning her white gaze from the thing at her feet.

'Homer,' I told her, 'describes the Laestrigones as cannibals.' She appeared too distressed to respond and rode on ahead.

This morning George looked for me. I see little of him these days, his duties being heavy and his leather apron much stained. He very kindly asked if I was well. I replied quite well, and thanked him.

'Myrtle says you've not been quite yourself. I understand there was an incident yesterday – '

'It was the pony that got bit,' I said. 'Not I. Besides, Beatrice is always on hand to give comfort.'

He stared at me strangely. I smiled and assured him I wasn't suffering from delusions, just that thinking of Beatrice kept me sane. I knew what troubled him – my failure to mention that portion of a limb stumbled upon by Myrtle. I could have told him that I'd heard the rain drumming on the stony path and that it sounded a death rattle in my ears. I could have described the peculiar angle of the toes ... but then, if it were within my powers to coolly and dispassionately deliberate on such things, as he undoubtedly must, seeing he spends his days gazing on similar horrors, my life might be easier and my speech less guarded.

As it is, severe self-control is necessary if I am to avoid being mastered by the impressions of the moment. This is what Horace meant when he advised we should study carefully that which will best promote a tranquil state of mind. I must bear and forbear and not wish things to be other than they are. Which is why I am engaged in contemplating my earlier existence, with a view to tracing whether chance or fate has brought me to this dreadful place at this particular moment in history.

Thus – on hearing the rough dialect of some Scottish infantryman about the camp, I dwell on childhood connections to his homeland. Though Manchester born, my father acted occasionally as an agent for the Leith Glassworks, in which capacity he was required to sail from one Hebridean station to another in search of kelp. On returning home from

[151]

one such tour he brought with him a toy four-wheeled cart made of tin and drawn by wooden horses. Before I was put to bed I had dismantled the cart into its various pieces. It was an act propelled by curiosity, rather than a destructive urge; I was anxious to learn how the pieces fitted together. I cannot remember whether I was whipped for it, though I suspect not as my father was a kind man.

It was in Scotland that I first showed an aptitude for geology, the shores of Cromarty being strewn with water-rolled fragments of primary rock derived from the west during the ages of boulder clay. On successive visits during my boyhood I took a diligent delight in sauntering over the pebble beds shaken up by the frequent storms. I took Beatrice to the spot some two years after we were married and attempted to interest her in the generic character of the porphyries, granites, gneisses, quartz rocks, mica-schists, etc., which littered the beach. Alas, there was an unfortunate encounter with a crustacean, which she swore had nipped her ankle, although I saw no sign of a mark. Result – we returned to our lodgings in silence.

No sooner had George gone back to his odious work than Myrtle came to ask if I would help tend her pony. I have no doubt it was at George's suggestion. The animal's wound was not serious; there are horses in far worse straits, and men too, for that matter.

Myrtle is an interesting subject – in regard to the question as to whether fate or chance holds the upper hand. The ifs are numerous. If Beatrice had not shown an affection for her, would she not have vanished into the orphanage? What if Pompey Jones's unfortunate arrangement of the tiger's head had not ended Annie's hopes of motherhood? If old Mrs Hardy had woken that morning in a cheerful mood, would Myrtle have been required to follow George down to the town? Then there is the matter of his returning to Blackberry Lane by a different route than was usual. If the woman's screams had echoed unheard in another street, what then? And if Mr Hardy had been confined to the blue room with a cold–

Perhaps chance and destiny are interdependent, in that the latter cannot be fulfilled without the casual intervention of the former. A craggy rock placed at a distance from water will never be worn smooth.

'Myrtle,' I began, 'you were attached to George right from a child, were you not?'

'I was,' she said.

'But why?'

'Why did you become attached to Beatrice?' she countered, and flashing me a glance of good-humoured malice, added, 'She was often cruel to you. I've seen her hit you.'

'I had reached an age when a man should be married. And besides, possibly it is in my nature to gain satisfaction from being treated roughly.'

'It's not in mine,' she said, and instructed me to hold the pony's head firmly while she dabbed at its flank with a dampened rag.

'He's a good-looking man,' I mused. 'But that is not the sort of thing a child particularly notices.'

'Is it not?' she exclaimed. 'Why, a child is always more aware of beauty than an adult. They're not hindered by preconceptions.'

'Aware, certainly,' I agreed. 'But not susceptible.'

'Nonsense,' she said, and her mouth became sulky.

'Nor,' I went on, 'do I remember George taking an especial interest in you. At least, no more than the rest of us ... once your prattling days had passed.'

'Nor did he,' she said. 'But for one time, and that was enough.'

I urged her to explain, at which she stared at me defiantly. She has a strong face, the eyes deep set and grave. Some weeks back she'd cropped her hair to be rid of the lice and but for her dress might now be taken for a boy.

'It's you we should be talking about,' she said. 'Not me.'

It was then I lost my temper and called her impertinent. Which was unfair of me. It was George I should have been angry with, not her. She stood, rag in hand, the defiance quite gone out of her, her eyes more mournful than ever. Dear God, I thought, how we have misused this poor child. But for chance she might have become a parlourmaid or the respectable wife of an honest working man.

That evening I was delighted to accompany George to the quarters of a Captain Jerome. His aunt had sent him a hamper of food, and, having reason to be grateful to George for curing an irritation of the bowel, he was generous enough to wish to share his good fortune. Myrtle wasn't included. She remained in the company of a motherly woman who has both a husband and son in the Light division. It was thought impolite to ask one woman without the other – also it would have meant less to eat all round.

As it was, two other gentlemen joined us, Captain Frampton of the 57th and a young lieutenant named Gormsby who had been involved in the skirmish at the Alma. I found the latter a highly nervous individual, wholly lacking in confidence; he could hardly hold his fork for the tremor in his hand and twice he spilt his wine.

The captain was fortunate to live within the four walls of a dilapidated one-storey house some quarter-mile from the camp. True, its windows were gone and there were several buckets placed about the floor to catch the rain dripping through the holes in the roof, but we dined at a proper table, albeit rickety, and the chair I sat on had a fair amount of upholstery.

The talk was mostly about war, in particular of the initial lack of support given to the Light division by the 1st division under the command of the Duke of Cambridge. Apparently the Duke was inexperienced. It was only after dangerous dithering that the Grenadiers and the Coldstream Guards reassembled and successfully routed the Russians.

I took no part in this discussion. How could I? All this talk of brigades and divisions and regiments considerably fuddles my mind. Nor did I care to add to the comments on the recent flogging of a rifleman for being drunk on guard duty. He should have received seventy lashes but collapsed after no more than fifty, it later being found that he had a fragment of ball-shot lodged in his back from the previous night's encounter with the enemy. George had attended him and said he would likely survive, though much diminished in both mind and body. I endeavoured to fill my head with other things and fancied I saw Beatrice in the candlelight, pursing her lips censoriously at the manner in which

I shovelled down my food. If she had been seated next to me I don't doubt she would have snatched up bits for herself, particularly when Auntie's plum pudding was served.

I was on happier ground, if not for long, when Captain Jerome pondered on the likelihood of our being home by Christmas. He had a house in Ireland with very extensive stables and much missed his string of horses. Damn fool that he was – his estimation – he had brought out one of his favourite mounts, Diabolo, as far as Kalamita Bay, where it had sickened and died. No obvious cause; but then, how could a creature so refined, so bred for perfection, survive such conditions? He felt its loss keenly, and had stood for an hour or more on the beach watching it float out to sea. He had every expectation of meeting this miraculous animal in the next world, though he earnestly hoped their reunion would be delayed for some years yet. I tried to look suitably affected at this nonsense, and failed. Such mawkishness offends me.

'It was Plato,' I ventured, 'who held quadrupeds to be a form of deteriorated humanity and essentially brutal.' Even as the words leapt from my mouth I regretted them: Jerome's brow was thunderous. I was saved by young Gormsby, mute until now, stammering out, 'There is no more brutal a species than man.'

Jerome toyed with his glass and looked immensely gloomy. Captain Frampton, who long since had fallen under the table, emitted a long, weary sigh. Outside, the low growl of the heavy guns on the heights above the ravine rolled through the night. Inside, the raindrops plop-plopped into the buckets.

At last, I said, 'You are acquainted, I am sure, with the myth of Athens waging war against a city founded by Neptune on the island of Atlantis – '

'We are not,' said George, 'but I'm sure you will tell us – '

'The gods allowed a great victory, after which both victors and vanquished were swallowed up by an earthquake and the island sank beneath the sea.'

'And what are we supposed to deduce from that?' asked Captain Jerome, watching the spin of an insect about the candle flame.

'Why,' I replied, 'that Mr Gormsby is in the right of it. We are a despicable species and deserve the punishment meted out by the gods.'

George and I took our leave at midnight, on foot. There was no moon and we jostled against each other in the darkness, our boots squelching mud.

'Potter,' George said, 'is it simply thoughtlessness, or is it your intention to give offence?'

'Offence – '

'Have you not the sensitivity to understand that these men are on nodding terms with death?'

'It is my sensitivity,' I replied agitatedly, 'that will not allow me to contemplate what is happening. I am not like you. You have spent years up to your elbows in blood – '

'There's no need to shout. I am not deaf – '

'To you the body is a mere composition of flesh and sinew. You care nothing for the brain – '

'The brain,' he said, 'equally disintegrates when met by force. It is no more durable than the rest of us.'

'I am a man accustomed to pass the hours in the reading

of books,' I cried. Stumbling, I would have fallen but for the support of his arm. 'I am a man accustomed to sleeping against the curve of his wife's back – '

'Women, 'George muttered. 'Always women.'

There lies the barrier between us. I have never understood his aversion to the female sex, beyond the burden of love his mother placed upon him. One should never forget the degeneracy that preceded the fall of Rome. As a product of a modern society I am persuaded that the union of the opposite sexes is desirable, not only in regard to the continuation of the race, but for its beneficial effect on the *soul*. My argument is admittedly weak, since I am far from convinced of the existence of such a spiritual organ. I had deluded myself into thinking that Myrtle's seduction of George – it can be couched no other way, for it was she who invaded his room that moon-dappled night – had swung him round. The chance arrival at Varna of Pompey Jones, breathing out fire, and my unannounced entry into the hospital tent in search of a stomach powder, put paid to the notion.

From somewhere to our right came the noise of tramping feet and the clank of shovels; the picquets were going out. The tiny spark of a spent cigarette sailed through the blackness and a voice called, 'Damn this rain. I shan't be surprised if we turns into fishes.'

Bad news awaited George. Word had got through that William Rimmer was dead of a head wound. As always, it was supposed he had not suffered. The shot had hit him fair and square between the eyes and snuffed him out like a candle.

*

Pompey Jones has shown up again, this time solely in charge of the photographer's van. His superior is not with him and he boasts of being on an important assignment for the Royal College of Surgeons, namely the obtainment of studies featuring wounds sustained by both the living and the dead. This, of course, requires him to spend his time in the company of George, though sometimes I have spied Myrtle and him involved in conversation. The van is somewhat the worse for wear, a shell having landed nearby and showered it with fragments. I caught Myrtle patting its sides as though it was an animal that needed calming. Two of the windows have gone and the paintwork is much scored, revealing streaks of purple and a curious golden letter, either U or N.

We are to move shortly, further up the Tchernaya valley towards a place known as Inkerman. I believe I visited this spot in happier days, for I recall ruins of the same name upon the mountainous heights.

Not wishing to be in the dark as to both the purpose and direction of our journey, I was forced to enquire of Captain Jerome where exactly we were heading. Beyond stating that we were to form part of the British siege corps to the right of Sebastopol, he was of little help, but reluctantly lent me a Russian map of the area. As far as I could tell the ridge called Inkerman is separated on the west by the Careenage Ravine and though forested to the east is open and bare to the west.

This, of course, means that we shall yet again be at the mercy of the elements.

I am in two minds as to whether I should bother to pack my tent, it being in a wretched state, perfectly sodden and much holed. It would be better for my health if I slept in the hospital tent, though that too is in a deplorable condition. I am at least better off as far as transport is concerned; three days ago over two hundred cavalry horses of the Light Brigade stampeded into the camp, their riders having perished in a charge along the north valley.

An auction was held, and I bought another mare so shocked by its recent subjection to bombardment as to have passed beyond nervousness into a state bordering on imbecility, and therefore manageable. Ear-drums shattered, she responds well enough to a prod of my boot. I turned loose the wicked little beast I had previously owned and have not seen her since.

Most mornings I forage for wood for the fire. The ground hereabouts, though stony, in places sprouts scrub oak. Although the stunted trees have long since been hacked down, the roots of some remain twisted within the earth. One would think the rain would make digging easier – not so, for the ground slopes precipitously and I am obliged to carry a pickaxe.

The other day, riding up the hillside bent on this monotonous task, I was near witness to an act of uncommon bravery, though many would regard it differently. A soldier – difficult to tell his age, for all except the very young are now equally sunken of eye and hollow of cheek – stood leaning against a boulder looking down at his feet. I did notice he was holding his rifle the wrong way round and thought perhaps he might be waiting for some edible creature to crawl out of the earth.

I had gone only a short distance when I heard the sound of a shot, followed by groaning. Riding back, I found the man standing on one leg, the other bent at the knee. There was a jagged hole in his boot, out of which bubbled a quantity of blood. Neither of us spoke for some moments, then, looking at me piteously, he asked, 'Did you see what happened, sir?'

'No,' I replied. 'I was some way ahead.'

'My hand must have slipped, sir – '

'No doubt from tiredness,' I said. 'One loses concentration.'

'That's it, sir,' he said eagerly. 'Me mind was on other things.'

I helped him into the saddle and led the mare down the hillside. He spoke to me of home and how he had been a pie-seller to the public houses around Hoxton. The pies were made by his father and sold for a penny, and were of better quality than most, though full of pepper to disguise what meat was used. He carried the gravy in an oil can, and when he'd made a sale he stuck his finger in the crust and poured the gravy into the hole. He was eighteen years old next birthday and he'd had sisters, none of whose faces he could remember because they'd died before he was grown. No, he wasn't in pain; leastways no worse than when he'd had an abscess beneath his tooth.

Would it, I pondered, have been less an act of cowardice if he had shot himself in the temple rather than the foot? In similar circumstances, would I have been able to muster the courage to injure myself? I decided not. I took him straightways to George, saying I'd found him lying in a ditch.

This morning, before we were due to move camp, a funeral service was held. Wood being so scarce the carpenters make few caskets and those only for the officers; the rest of the dead are wrapped in old tents or pieces of oil-cloth and laid side by side on bullock carts seized from the surrounding villages.

The burial ground, once an orchard, lay in a hollow a short distance away. Out of respect for the occasion, the gods had stilled the rain and the sun sent forth a weak glitter. When the wagons began their lurching progression over the stony ground, the makeshift shrouds shook loose and it was noticeable how many of the corpses were going barefooted to the grave. Some among us hissed their disapproval at the sight, possibly the very ones who now walked better shod than before. I myself did not find it objectionable; as the chaplain presently intoned, *We brought nothing into this world, and it is certain we carry nothing out. The Lord gave, and the Lord hath taken away.*

Pompey Jones set up his tripod and put on his hood. There is something of black magic in the photographer's art, in that he stops time. The chaplain left off reading and stayed motionless with the book in his hand, the men stood bareheaded; only the poor dead stirred as the winding cloths flapped in the wind.

I don't know that I think much of the camera. It appears to hold reality hostage, and yet fails to snap thoughts in the head. A man can be standing there, face expressive of grief, and inside be full of either mirth or lust. The lens is power-less to catch the interior turmoil boiling within the skull, nor can it expose lewd recollections – which is all to the good. In my case, staring transfixed at the wrapped dead, I con-ceived an image of Beatrice in her weekend night-gown. At bedtimes, no doubt stirred by a Sunday morning spent dwelling on the hereafter, she was in the habit of taking the initiative, clambering over me, breath smelling of chocolate pudding, thighs reeking of that exciting odour of crayfish.

The rain fell again. *Man that is born of woman hath but a short time to live, and is full of misery. He cometh up, and is cut down like a flower; he fleeth as it were a shadow –*

It was then, standing there, my eyes fixed on the row of mummies about to be consigned to the mud, that I saw Beatrice. She was beckoning me. I closed my lids, thinking to blot her out, but she was still there, finger crooked. I obeyed her, though reluctantly. She floated ahead, and stopping beside an outcrop of rock gestured me to kneel down. There, in a crevice, waved a thin stalk crowned with a blue flowerhead no larger than a bodice button. I looked up, and Beatrice was smiling, and the smile was full of love. I reached out my hand and plucked the flower and she shook her head sorrowfully. No, no, I heard her say, but her voice was gentle, the tone a mother uses to a child. Behind me, the chaplain was reciting, *Blessed are the dead that die in the Lord; even so sayeth the Spirit; for they rest from their labours.* Then Beatrice left me and the dead were dropped into the ground to begin their dissolution. I opened my fist and the wind tore away that scrap of blue crumpled within my palm. I thought of Mr Lyell and his supposition that the human race faced not merely extinction but the gradual obliteration of every trace of its existence.

Afterwards, when we'd marched back again, George demanded to know why I'd behaved so disrespectfully. He said I'd picked the wrong moment to show off my knowledge of rocks. I didn't defend myself.

I rode towards Inkerman with my chin buried in my shirt, smelling myself for warmth. A man can vomit from the stench given off by others, yet take positive pleasure in the odour produced by himself. Midst the dirt and the staleness I detected the frail scent of cornflowers.

Plate 6. November 1854

SMILE, BOYS, SMILE

We are positioned on a ridge above the Tchernaya valley opposite some ruins. Potter says the stones are very ancient. He now remembers visiting the spot when a young man, and tells of a monastery built into the rock. He rambles on about medieval times, which I take to be some years into the past.

With the exception of the troops who guard our headquarter camps and the French ports of supply, our army, starting from Stresleka Bay, spreads out in a line twenty miles long, runs parallel with the Sebastopol defences until it reaches the Careenage Ravine, enfolds half Mount Inkerman, then doubles back southward along the crest of the Sapouné Ridge.

I glean all this from Potter, who has pestered a Captain Frampton for information. We are apparently sat between Sir Richard England's division and General Buller's brigade. The 21st, under Sir George Cathcart – we haven't yet set eyes on him – is mainly engaged in manning the trenches. Should Lord Raglan be forced to call for reinforcements to defend Mount Inkerman, we'd have to march two and a half miles across country. I say *we*, though I don't intend to budge.

From our ridge there is a view of the ravine and the Post road which winds towards Sebastopol. Weather permitting and with a fair amount of squinting I can make out the extremities of the harbour, slashed by the masts of ships and the stretch of water that Potter refers to as 'the Gateway to the Mediterranean'. That bleak gap is apparently the reason for all this misery. As sea and sky are the same ashen shade of grey it is difficult to think of it leading anywhere upon which the sun might shine.

Potter has become something of an expert on military strategy. He spends hours scratching arrows in the mud, indicating possible sorties from the enemy. George doesn't like it; whenever he catches him he pretends he hasn't seen the marks and smears them under his boot. The other afternoon, following an obliteration, Potter cried out, '*Likeness is none between us, but we go to the self-same end.*' George strode off looking thunderous.

Each morning, at first light, two squads of picquets march out to relieve those of the night watch. A picquet is composed of an entire company, and as the casualties increase, often the poor devils stay in their mud-filled trenches in excess of forty-eight hours. They return, some still clothed in their once bright summer uniforms – now turned the colour of old beetroot – dragging their feet and with faces old as time. There is little difference between the living and the dead, save that the latter come back on litters.

The din goes on day and night, though at some distance. I've got used to it. Nor do I start back in fear any more when the grey horizon flashes with violet light and throws up fiery plumes. Often the smoke assumes the shapes of ghostly ridges which tremble for a while, turn pink, then melt into the sullen sky. I've seen a dwarf oak catch fire and blaze in the night like Moses's burning bush. The explosions throw up stones which, falling, rearrange themselves in burial mounds.

I intend to survive. I consulted Potter and he agreed with me that a man, so long as he keeps concentration, can will himself into staying alive. I'm not like those other wretched examples of my class who come from nothing, and who, should they escape the slaughter, are doomed to return to the same oblivion, and be broken men into the bargain.

I have it planned out. I shall rise in my profession, wed a good woman without airs or graces, and grow old surrounded by my children. I don't hanker to be over-rich, just comfortable. None of my offspring, God willing, will ever beg for bread as I once did.

With this in mind, and the photographer having found himself a billet outside the camp, I've taken to sleeping in the van, to be out of the damp. I claim it as my own vehicle, seeing it was me who purchased it, the Punch and Judy man having died and gone to his maker. It was also my idea to put in tinted windows and build shelves, though I regret painting the outside white as it can be seen for miles and often draws fire. It's cramped, and at nightfall I turf some of the chemicals outside, which wouldn't please my employer if he came back unexpected. If he does, I'm all set to ask him whether he wants a live assistant or a dead one, the condition of the tents being guaranteed to shove one into the grave. Supplies can't get through owing to the constant barrage from the Russian guns; there is only one blanket

apiece and that so encrusted with slime from the waterlog-
ged earth as to be useless. The men who doze within such
musty shelters pile together for warmth, stirring and jostling like a litter of pigs.

Potter and Myrtle have moved inside the hospital tent
with George, though that has become no better than a char-
nel house. Not a day goes by without its quota of wounded.
One night, in the space of three hours, ten men were
brought in, felled by a howitzer shell. Of these, seven had
already lost either an arm or a leg and the remaining three
required amputations.

At first Dr Potter used to go outside when George began
his sawing. Now he stays put by the stove, pretending to be
absorbed in one of his mildewed books.

There's no telling who will live and who will not. A man
can have his limbs torn off, the blood draining out of him
like a leaking barrel, and recover; another can stumble in
with no more than a flesh wound to the groin and snuff it
within twenty-four hours. Those whose stomachs have
been ploughed up, their innards dangling like pale links of
pork, fare the worst. Neither will-power nor medicine can
heal them.

They carried in a drummer boy a few nights back. He was
not above twelve years of age and had been put to work in
the trenches, there being so many casualties. In the act of
shovelling up dirt, body bent and his right hand holding the
handle of the spade, he was struck by a round shot which
passed between his legs, laid bare an artery and ripped off
his cock and scrotum. They hadn't been able to bring him in
right away owing to the ambulance wagon getting stuck in

the mud. He was put on the table, where he jerked like a fish on the hook. Myrtle didn't go near him. Potter says she's a devoted mother, but I suspect her children function as a cord to bind her more tightly to George.

Nothing could be done for the drummer boy. George told me to administer chloroform. I've taken to helping in this way, and am glad to be of use. If you know they're asleep and you see their faces smooth out, your belly stops heaving. I held the pad over the lad's face for a long time, so that he never woke again, not in this world. The chloroform smells fruity, a touch like strawberries, which is pleasant since we all stink, Potter more than most.

I've reminded George of the time he and William Rimmer had me go into the cage with the ape, and how he'd been drunk as a lord on the journey home to Blackberry Lane. I reckon memory is selective because he held it was me who was inebriated, as proved by the way I'd stretched out in the sand while he was conversing with the fisher of eels. He didn't like my mentioning Rimmer; I could tell that from the way his eyelids fluttered.

Stung, I said, 'Rimmer was cock-a-hoop that day. He wanted to take all the credit.'

George said, 'I haven't your memory,' and turned his back on me.

I tried to get Potter to discuss what it meant when events were recollected differently. He said he wasn't in the mood and had enough lapses of his own without fretting over other people's. Often he talks to his wife Beatrice, which disturbs George. He fears Potter is going out of his mind. I detect no evidence of it, and besides, things being the way they are, removing oneself from the present, by whatever ruse, seems a sensible enough way of keeping cheerful. I try to think of someone I could conjure up should it become necessary, but there's no one. My mother's face got wiped clean in the long gone past.

When the drummer boy was laid down, Potter started mumbling aloud from one of his books. I shall follow his example and read when I get old. He himself once said I was half-way to being a scholar, seeing that the action of the camera goes some distance towards capturing the mystery of human conduct.

Before they buried the drummer boy I stripped him of his uniform and encouraged Myrtle to wear it. Her dress was too thin for the winter and in any case much bedraggled. She refused outright, but I got George to persuade her, and now she wears a jacket and breeches. She didn't even have to wash them, the blood having been rinsed off by the rain. All that was needed was a patch – in this case, a square of red petticoat – to cover the holes torn in the trousers. She looks well in such clothes and I would like to take her portrait, only it pours all the time and the plates would get splattered.

Most nights, when there's a lull in the hacking and suturing, we huddle round the stove. There are usually five of us. I've chummed up with an elderly man called Charles White. He hails from Ireland and is good-humoured. Starting out poor, he made a fortune out of brick fields but was later ruined owning to a failure of the bank. Unused to penury, his wife faded away and now lies in a pauper's grave. He himself, until war was declared and he volunteered for military service, was incarcerated in the debtors' under-ground prison in Clerkenwell. In spite of this he jokes a good deal. He has a ginger moustache and walks with his feet splayed out. George finds him amusing and has suc-cessfully reduced a swelling of the ankles caused by his former shackling.

White was telling one of his tall tales when a soldier bounded in with his ear blown off. There was any amount of blood but he wouldn't let George see to him. He kept shaking our hands in turn and saying how happy he was to meet us. His name was Harry St Claire, a name he recited over and over, as though it had value. He said losing his ear was the best thing that had ever happened to him. White thought this meant he was under the delusion that he would now be sent home, and assured him that he'd be back on duty within two days, at which the poor wretch cried out, 'Capital, capital,' and did another round of handshaking, the blood flying in all directions as he pumped.

His story was a strange one, and being educated he told it well. Some months before, as yet he was not sure how many, he had been a pupil at a school of high repute in the south of England. As clear as he could remember – there was a blue sky and the college cat was stalking the bushes – he had taken umbrage over a fellow of his own age speaking disrespectfully of his mother, a widow woman recently keeping company with a titled gentleman. Mad to defend his mother's honour, he had challenged the youth to fisti-cuffs beneath the chestnut trees at the boundary of the playing fields. It went badly for him. In his head he'd retained an image of the cat, the sunlight shivering across its brindled fur; that and the sparkles of his own sweat darkening the hairs on his arm. Then the blackness descended.

Weeks later, he had found himself enlisted and on a ship bound for Malta. He hadn't the slightest idea of who he was or where he had come from. When required to give his name he had said he didn't know it, at which he had been written down as Private Knowlitt. This tickled Charles White, who laughed himself into a fit of coughing.

An hour ago, marching back from picquet duty, a shell had landed in the rear of the column and an iron fragment had sliced off Knowlitt's ear. At the moment of impact – he had dived through the air like a swimmer – he had remembered his name and his former life. 'I am Harry St Claire,' he had called out, and now repeated the information, adding, 'I am the happiest man alive.'

Suddenly, his face whitened. From outside, like the beating of wings, came the dull clapping of the guns. He stared into the distance, his eyes grown huge. Then he dropped dead. George said it was due to exhaustion, that and blood loss.

Myrtle took it hard. She sat with her knees splayed wide, hands held in front of her, tapping the air with invisible sticks, as though the drummer boy had come back to claim his soul. Potter curled up on his stool, hands covering his ears.

White and I slung Knowlitt between our shoulders and dragged him outside. His dead man's boots slurped through the mud. A fearful detonation cracked the darkness, followed by a flash of sickly light, exposing for an instant the tin glitter of the river below and the slopes sluiced with rain. The world was drowning.

I didn't go back to George. Instead, I tumbled into the van and got at the photographer's reserves of Bulgarian wine.

*

I woke early, the drink having dragged me awake with a dry mouth. I had a cloudy memory of keeping company with a corporal of the 55th with a boil on his neck. He had been willing to swap a watch for a pigskin valise. The watch had gone and there was no sign of the valise, which brought me out of my stupor with a vengeance. I had a small heap of trophies plucked from corpses, wrapped in a cloth and stuffed behind the developing trays. My conscience doesn't trouble me. The enemy rifle the bodies after an engagement and I reckon I'm doing our dead a service by keeping their possessions out of foreign hands.

I stepped down into a fog as thick as wool. The customary stand-to had begun, but though I could hear the shouted orders and the whinnying of horses, it was impossible to see anything. If I stretched out my arm and held up my hand, my fingers vanished. I was caught in a white bale of mist, through which I heard the solemn ringing of church bells. I reckoned the sound drifted up from Sebastopol and that I had woken on a saint's day, either that or it was Sunday. Stumbling forwards, I came across a lumpen form slumped before a ghostly leap of flame. It was Potter, swaddled in his greatcoat at the fire, waiting for the pot to simmer. I tapped his shoulder and said, 'Just listen to those bells.'

[175]

He said, 'You hear them too? I thought they were in my head. I woke dreaming of my wedding day. Beatrice had a speck of soot on the edge of her veil – '

'Dear me,' I said. 'She wouldn't take too kindly to that.'

'Was it the bells that caused the dream,' he pondered, 'or had the dream already begun and I merely incorporated the sound?'

I said I would have to leave that question unanswered.

'I presume you were never married,' he probed. 'You not being the marrying sort.'

I told him he presumed rightly, but that I'd lived for two years with a widow woman, until the drink had bloated her out and scuttled my desire.

'You surprise me,' he said.

'I surprise myself,' I countered, and asked after Myrtle.

'She cried herself into sleep, and must now be her old self.'

'Hardly old,' I corrected.

He agreed I had a point, and fell silent. I thought that was the end of it, but he presently asked, 'What was it that George did all those years ago … to make her love him?'

'Did?' I said. I felt uncomfortable, love not being a word I care to bounce about. I told him he should ask George, not me.

'He won't remember,' Potter said. 'It's not as if he's a man swayed by emotion.'

It hit me that he wasn't as clever as I'd believed; either that or his old books had finally clamped him tight between their pages. I know about men, and knew George to be softer than most. He could cry like a woman at the mention of his mother.

I said, 'Possibly he told her where she came from.'

'Would that be enough?' He sounded unconvinced. His face kept slipping in and out of the mist.

'What more would be needed?' I asked. 'It's useful to know one's beginnings.'

'There are more urgent things to contemplate,' he muttered, 'one's end for instance,' and the water having come to the boil, made tea. We drank it to the clump of boots as the fatigue detail set off on the dawn search for wood and water. Close by, a horse pissed, its splatterings diminishing as it trotted on.

'These are times in which the truth should be told,' Potter announced portentously. 'Do you not think so, Pompey Jones?'

'What truth would that be?' I asked. His face had vanished again.

'In this case,' he said, 'I'm speaking of pictures.'

I thought he meant photographs, and told him straight that I couldn't see eye to eye with him. 'Some pictures,' I confided, 'would only cause alarm to ordinary folk.' I was thinking of the studies of exit wounds taken for the College of Surgeons.

'I had in mind,' he said, 'a view of ships in the Mersey, seen from the hill on which the Washington Hotel now stands.'

He had me utterly confused. Perhaps, after all, George had been in the right of it when he'd held that Potter was leaving his mind.

'You may remember it hung on the wall in the study,' he continued. 'It was moved some weeks before you were barred from the house.'

It was true I'd been banned from visiting Blackberry Lane, though that hadn't stopped George from seeing me. One night he'd sent a note to my lodgings asking me to meet him on the north side of the Washington Hotel. I'd had every intention of complying, but when I strode down the hill I'd glimpsed yellow flames rolling through the sky above the river. When I reached the Custom House, the blazing sails of ships skimmed like kites across the crimson waters, and it hurt to breathe. Even at this distance in time I recalled the howl of the fire as it hurtled towards the stars. When the tobacco warehouse collapsed and the sparks sprayed out in ostrich feathers, the crowd had burst out cheering. It wasn't just the conflagration that had prevented me from keeping my appointment with George – it rankled that he'd stipulated the kitchen entrance rather than the front steps of the hotel. I was finished with being consigned to the shadows. Next morning he was waiting for me by the pump in my street. He'd given me one of his old cameras which I sold later that day for sixteen shillings, as I had a better one of my own.

Potter said, 'First it was positioned above the desk. You may recollect a blue vase with a fluted neck that stood below it. Then it was found askew on the wall to the right of the door.'

Flummoxed, I uttered not a word.

'I stayed up two nights ... in an effort to solve the mystery. I was not then a man used to going without sleep. In the scale of things it is of small importance, yet I would be grateful for an explanation.'

'I can't help you,' I said, and left him.

Once inside the van I set about smartening the shelves in case the photographer returned. Though I had been careful in my handling of the glass plates and the positives, the numerous bottles were in a jumble and the trays not sufficiently clean. The thief who had sat with me the night before had slopped drink on to the work bench. After storing the chemicals in a more orderly fashion I inspected the cameras, of which there were three, one being for portraits and fitted with a Ross three-inch lens, the others of the bellows construction and made by Bourquien of Paris.

Two of the prints were all my own work and I considered them pretty fair examples of the photographer's art. The first was a study of a heap of amputated limbs; arrayed against a white background, they had the gravity of a still-life. I was pleased with the tuft of grass spraying up from a clenched fist. The second was of the funeral ceremony held in the region we had recently quitted. Removing this second print from its waxed wrappings I examined it for fading. It was acute, the white vestments of the chaplain and the winding cloths of the dead standing out against the stony landscape. Possibly there was a little blurring in the left-hand corner, but it was scarcely noticeable.

And then, even as I looked, it became so, and gradually assumed the shape of a woman. The more I stared, the clearer it grew, until I couldn't think why I hadn't seen it in the first place. It puzzled me, for we weren't encouraged to have women in the pictures, not unless they were ladies,

[179]

and we hadn't any of those, and besides, it was thought that people back home don't like to see the weaker sex in such grim surroundings. I was certain there had been only three women present, one being Myrtle, and all had been grouped well to the rear of the camera. The shape was bulky, matronly; bonnet-strings hung down quite clearly and one hand appeared raised, either waving or beckoning.

I stood there, trying to make sense of it, when an uproar began outside. I opened the doors and the noise of bellowed commands and the tooting of bugles rushed in with the fog. Someone called my name, and peering, I made out the outline of a boy standing there. When the figure came closer I saw it was Myrtle.

'What's up?' I asked.

'George needs you,' she said. 'There's been orders to march.'

I tried to persuade her inside the van, to be out of the way of the unseen horses and the invisible soldiery running to stand-to. She wouldn't, protesting it would remind her too much of old Mr Hardy. I thought it was other things she was loath to remember, like the dreams she'd once had of George forsaking all others, so I stepped down into the swirling day and followed her to the hospital tent.

Potter was there, helping to carry medical boxes to the ambulance wagons, of which there were two, one being nothing more than a bullock cart. The talk was that Prince Mentschikoff had launched a surprise attack on the 2nd division and we were required to give support. The bells earlier that morning had tolled to spur on the Russian battalions swarming out of Sebastopol. The strength of the enemy force was rumoured to be immense. Some said that as many as forty thousand men were on the advance.

George started on me at once, issuing orders and telling me to look sharp. I was annoyed, for I was present in a civilian capacity and had neither wish nor obligation to enter the firing line. I told myself I'd go with him a short way and then double back, and later make the fog my excuse.

As it happened, there was only one driver, a bandsman, who could be spared to take charge of the ambulance wagon, George himself having made up his mind to go on ahead to find a suitable place to set up a field hospital. Imperiously, he directed me to the bullock cart – Potter being useless in such matters – and, instrument bag propped before him in the saddle, rode off before I had time to protest.

It took time to get on our way, what with the confusion and the lack of visibility. When finally we were ready Myrtle clambered up beside me. Potter couldn't find his horse; instead, he hung a lantern on the back of the cart and said he would walk behind. Now we could hear the rumble of the heavy guns, theirs and ours, and closer, the staccato snap of musket fire coming from the slopes above the ravine.

Our progress was slow and lurching. The planks of wood laid down by the picquets had mostly been torn up to be used for firewood, and those that remained had long since sunk into the mud. In places the oak bushes grew thickly, impeding the wooden wheels of the cart. At intervals the mist cleared and the grey columns of marching men could be seen slipping and sliding through the grey daylight.

Myrtle was trembling. I told her not to be afraid, and she retorted angrily that it was cold not fear that made her teeth rattle. Occasionally she shouted out to see if Potter was keeping up, and for perhaps an hour we heard his called response. Then he didn't answer any more, and I reckoned he'd turned back or else lost his way.

Frequently, Myrtle urged me to go faster, and even leaned dangerously forwards, pummelling her feather fists against the rump of the stumbling horse in a vain attempt to make it speedier. She wanted to find George. I wasn't against it, for now I reckoned the hell that awaited was in some degree preferable to the one left behind; at least I wouldn't be alone.

I tried to make an adventure of it, pretending I was a child again, sneaking through Ince Woods hoping to snare rabbits, but the trees were too small and the frantic crack of the guns blew away the black crows of my boyhood.

Once, when the fog shifted to reveal a fountain of flame spurting upon the horizon, I conjured up the sunset spreading across the sky beyond the humpbacked bridge, and in the puffs of gory smoke belching along the rise imagined I glimpsed the eucalyptus leaves quivering above the stream.

Dreaming thus, suddenly there came a crackling and tearing of undergrowth somewhere to our right, and there burst into view a triangle of men in greatcoats and bearskins, rifles held at the hip, bayonets fixed. Then broke out a clamour of such ferocity that my eyes started in my head. I thought it was all up with me, for above the frenzied grunting and shouting and caterwauling came the whine of shot. The cart trundled on, the horse straining and panting to be out of the din.

It was over in less than a minute and we were through it, unharmed, and it grew quiet again, as though a door had slammed shut. It might have been a dream, but for the bodies lying all around. When I turned to look back I saw one of our Fusiliers sitting upright in the mud, eyes wide open and the top of his head sliced off like he was a breakfast egg. Behind him stood a Russian holding a pistol at arm's length; it was aimed at my heart. Even as his finger tightened on the trigger the cart lurched sideways and toppled over, flinging me into the bushes. Miraculously, Myrtle fell alongside.

After what seemed like hours I lifted my head and peered through the fretwork of branches. The seated soldier had fallen on to his back and the Russian had gone. Then the firing and the shouting began again, but this time at a distance. My lids were clamped shut but still the detonations flashed behind my eyes.

I stretched out and pulled Myrtle close. Quiet as a mouse she curled against me. Her cap had come off and her hair, stiff with dirt, spiked my cheek. I didn't succeed in penetrating her. She let me stroke her cleft but bridled when I attempted greater intimacies. I didn't persist, it not being a matter of importance. All I'd ever wanted, as regards Myrtle, was the recognition that she and I were of a kind, seeing that fate had tumbled the two of us into Master Georgie's path.

After a while I stood and tugged her upright. Magpies

swooped about our heads. The mist had all but cleared and drizzle spattered the ground. The horse lay on its side, haunches pinned down by the cart. It was still alive though I suspected both its hind legs were broken. I loosened the fingers of the dead fusilier and took up his rifle. When I placed the muzzle against the animal's forehead Myrtle turned away. The gun didn't go off; possibly the powder was wet. Searching through the other corpses I chanced on a revolver and dispatched the horse without further delay. I decided to keep the rifle too, for its bayonet was in place and I reckoned that in close combat steel was superior to lead.

A dozen or more Russians were spilled round the cart. I opened the coat of one to see if there was anything of value inside, but Myrtle was watching me, so I tugged it off altogether and struggled into its folds. There was a leathery smell and the homely odour of sweat. For good measure I jerked free the metal canister that hung at his belt and downed his vodka ration in one swallow. For the first time that day the blood ran warm in my veins. I would have worn his bearskin too if I hadn't feared I might be mistaken for the enemy.

What to do next – that was the puzzle. For all I knew the Russians were in the rear as well as ahead. From the ridge a mile distant came the roar of cannons and the pitter-pat of musket fire. There was nothing to see from the top of the rise save for the sky burning red in patches. The fog still rolled across the valley, covering the road and the stone barrier. Beyond the unseen river, steep walls of rock jutted out of the mist and soared sheer to the ruins of Inkerman.

Myrtle settled it. She said, 'I'm going on. I have to find Georgie.'

I said, 'I doubt you'll ever find him.'

She shook her head stubbornly. 'I will ... I must.'

'He's probably dead by now,' I told her.

At this she fairly trembled with passion. 'He's not,' she ground out. 'I know he's not.'

Dollops of mud had dried across her face, lending her skin a ghastly pallor – yet her eyes glittered, as if she was greedy for something.

It was a grisly walk we took, by-stepping dead men and bits of men. There were wounded horses, heads lowered, standing with the blood leaking out of their bellies. I would have used the revolver if I hadn't felt it would be a feckless waste of ammunition. Once, we heard a groan and running in that direction came across a middle-aged man in the uniform of the Rifle Brigade. He lay on his back, hands clasped together as though in prayer, spectacles still balanced on his nose. There wasn't a mark on him, save that the glass at his right eye was fractured into a spider's web. He groaned again and I knelt and lifted his head, and at that precise moment his throat gave forth a death rattle. I withdrew my hand and it was sticky with bloody pulp. I wiped my fingers on his trousers and hurried on.

*

I left Myrtle in the siege camp below the ravine. I would have skulked there in her shadow if an officer hadn't come up and, taking me for a soldier, what with my greatcoat and rifle, ordered me to refill my ammunition pouch and proceed towards the Sandbag Battery. I had no notion of where that might be, but the drink had made me compliant. I gathered it was almost midday; I hadn't eaten since six o'clock the evening before, and that only bread gone mouldy with the damp.

I fell in with a column of the 4th division and duly marched off, watching torpedoes of fire blazing through the misty heavens, a silly smile on my face.

We toiled in an easterly direction towards a spur of rock encircled by a wall some ten foot high, erected from stones and fortified by burst sandbags. It had been fashioned in the hopes of trundling up heavy artillery, but was in fact empty. Quite why it was deemed necessary to defend such a nothing place was never explained. Our ascent along sheep tracks was enlivened by the whistle of shells streaking down from the Russian batteries, and had us bounding and weaving like hares.

Shortly, we were pounced on by Russians looming up in looking-glass reflections of ourselves, eyes dilated with horror, bearskins bristling like brushwood. It was hand to hand encounters and my bayonet proved its worth. After that first sickening thrust into flesh and muscle – I swear the steel conducted a discharge of agony – it became ordinary, commonplace, to pierce a man through the guts. I didn't look at faces, into fear-filled eyes, only at the width of the cloth protecting the fragile organs from the daggers of death.

I witnessed an extraordinary happening, a confrontation between an officer of the 21st and his equal on the enemy side. They went to it with swords, circling each other, apes on the prowl. At which their men, of both sides, formed a ragged ring about them, cheering and uttering oaths.

I stood at the back, watching the cut and thrust of their dance of death. When they fell, each mortally wounded, the circle broke up and hacked away with a vengeance.

I engaged with a boy with a pimple at the corner of his mouth. He was clumsy with terror, flicking at me with his bayonet as though warding off bees. He shouted something in a foreign tongue, and I said I was sorry but I didn't understand. I wanted to spare him, but he caught me a slash on my brow which got me cross and I jabbed him in the throat. He fell away, gurgling his reproach.

I didn't know what cause I was promoting, or why it was imperative to kill, though I reckon Potter could have told me.

The carnage was horrid. Men died posed like the statues in Mr Blundell's glass-house. I saw a horse crumpled on its chest, its rider with his arm held up as though he breasted a river. I saw two men on their knees, facing one another, propped up by the pat-a-cake thrust of their hands. On the wall, stuck to the steps of a ladder, a grenadier clutched at the steel that pinned him like a butterfly.

Soon an officer charged up on his horse and ordered us to retreat from the Battery to defend the Regimental Colours. In my head I questioned the necessity of coming to the aid of a tattered square of silk, but did as I was bid. I'd turned into a circus animal and would have jumped through hoops if called upon. As we ran down the slope the smoke from the guns whirled about us as though a giant kettle was on the boil.

We had to rush past the poor wretches surrounding the Colours and attack the Russians from behind. Those who were out of ammunition or had left their bayonets in flesh screamed like madmen and hurled stones and debris. Enemy reinforcements stole up and shot us in the back.

Impossible to say how long it lasted; time stood brutally still. There was a moment, staring down that avenue of slaughter, when I swear I saw Potter sauntering towards me. Behind him, a ball from a heavy pounder bounced in pursuit like a stone skimming water. I opened my mouth to shout a warning, and just as it leapt to tear him apart he swerved aside as though pushed; it hurtled on and took off the head of a man in front. I reckoned an angel kept watch over Potter.

I was still alive when it ended. The Russians retreated up the hillside, leaving their dead and wounded where they'd fallen. The cessation affected the living in different ways; some lay down and slept, others walked about in a trance, plucking at their faces. For myself, I shook all over and could barely stand. It was the silence that was unnerving.

I found George two hours later, plying his trade at the Quarry end of the valley, Myrtle at his side. He was bent over a man with a hole in his chest. I tapped his wrist and he glanced up and didn't know me, but then, so altered had we grown I only knew him by his blood-spattered apron. He took in the gash on my forehead and said dismissively, 'It's only a scratch. Move on.' Then I spoke his name and he sprang upright; for the first and last time he took me in his arms.

I helped dig trenches to bury the dead. The ones who had perished lying flat were dragged away by the heels. Those that sat upright we lifted under the arms, if arms remained. We found six men, comrades and foes, linked together, bayonets quivering in a daisy chain of steel.

George was fetched to see to an officer who had lost both feet, his stumps stuck in a barrel of gunpowder to staunch the bleeding. I was sent to find a stretcher and we laid him on it, barrel and all, and set off towards the hospital table, George leading. Myrtle followed, as she had always done.

We had got no more than twenty yards when Myrtle called out George's name. She said later that she'd hurt her foot on a stone. He stopped and wheeled round, still holding the stretcher. Behind him, a wounded Russian, propped against sandbags, lifted up his musket and fired. George let go of the stretcher and the barrel rolled away trailing grey powder. He was looking at me, eyes wide with surprise. 'You're a good boy,' I thought he said; then he fell down.

*

Potter was in the hospital tent when we arrived at the camp. He said he'd turned back earlier that morning owing to the fog settling on his chest. The photographer had returned and was preparing the plates. I was to hurry because the light was going.

I said, 'George is dead.'

'You've a cut on your forehead,' he replied, and tearing

some pages from the book on his knee, stuffed them into the stove.

Myrtle was outside, dry-eyed, cradling George in her arms. She was crooning to him.

I walked back to the van and found the photographer nearby with his camera set up and five men slouched before him.

'What we want,' he said, 'is a posed group of survivors to show the folks back home.' Squinting down the lens he called out, 'The balance isn't right. I need another soldier. Fetch one.'

I walked back to George. Myrtle had gone and he was lying in the mud. I humped him over my shoulder and carried him to the camera. The men were now standing and I propped him between them. He slumped forward and the soldier to his right supported him round the waist.

'Smile, boys, smile,' urged the photographer.

Behind, on the brow of the hill I saw Myrtle, arms stretched wide, circling round and round, like a bird above a robbed nest.